Frederick William Conrad

The CALL to the MINISTRY

Frederick William Conrad

The CALL to the MINISTRY

ISBN/EAN: 9783741122606

Manufactured in Europe, USA, Canada, Australia, Japa

Cover: Foto ©Andreas Hilbeck / pixelio.de

Manufactured and distributed by brebook publishing software
(www.brebook.com)

Frederick William Conrad

The CALL to the MINISTRY

THE PREVALENT AND TRUE THEORIES EXAMINED

BY F. W. CONRAD, D. D.

[FROM THE LUTHERAN QUARTERLY, OCTOBER, 1883.]

GETTYSBURG:

J. E. WIBLE, STEAM PRINTER, CARLISLE STREET (SECOND SQUARE).

1883.

THE CALL TO THE MINISTRY.

Jesus Christ represented the world under the similitude of a great field, in which a spiritual harvest is growing, wide in extent, priceless in value, ripe for the sickle, and ready to perish. The ability and willingness of the Lord of the harvest to send laborers into this harvest, and the duty of the Church to pray to him to call an adequate number to gather it, as well as to make the necessary efforts to induce those thus called to devote their lives to it, are both declared and enjoined in the word of God. Notwithstanding this, the disproportion between the number of the laborers and the extent of the harvest has continued for ages, and the moral results have proven most disastrous to mankind. Because the laborers were too few, much of the harvest of the world-field perished during the past; because their number is still inadequate, vast proportions of it are perishing now; and if no remedy has been devised and can be applied, the full harvest can never be gathered into the garner of heaven.

The questions accordingly arise: Must the laborers always be too few, and much of the harvest continue to perish? Has the Lord of the harvest been unwilling to call an adequate number of laborers, or has the Church entertained erroneous views concerning the call to the ministry, and failed to make the necessary efforts to induce those called to enter her service? To us it is manifest that the latter, and not the former, is the true cause of the inadequacy of the number of ministers to preach the Gospel according to the great commission of Christ to every creature. This we hope to establish by an examination of the prevalent and true theories concerning the call to the ministry.

THE PREVALENT THEORY STATED AND FOUND WANTING.

A theory embraces certain ideas, which operate as govering principles in practice. The ideas generally entertained concerning the call to the ministry, consequently, constitute the theory and influence the practice of the Church. According to the prevalent theory it is held that a call to the ministry emanates directly from God; that it is addressed to particular individuals; that the conviction of their call is impressed upon their minds in an extraordinary manner, through the immediate influence of the Holy Spirit; that these will be introduced into the ministry by the grace and providence of God; that those called are either in the ministry or else in a course of preparation for it; that few if any who have devoted themselves to other vocations and professions, were called to the ministry; that the number thus called is entirely inadequate to preach the unsearchable riches of Christ to the poor and famishing millions of the world; and that, however much the Church may regret this deficiency and mourn over the consequent ruin of souls, she is neither responsible for, nor able to remedy it.

As theory determines the practice of the Church, so, too, does her practice reveal her theory. Holding the views concerning the call to the ministry just expressed, and impressed by the danger of introducing uncalled men into the sacred office, she has not felt the weight of responsibility resting upon her; and deeming it best to withhold her hand from the subject, she has, to a great extent left the supply of ministers to the judgment of individuals, influenced by their own impulses and convictions of duty, believed to have been produced by the internal working of the Spirit, and corroborated by the external leadings of the providence of God. That this theory is erroneous, we trust will be demonstrated by a due consideration of the following arguments.

1. Because it is unreasonable. It is unreasonable to expect the attainment of an end without making ample provision of the means adapted to attain it. A husbandman who has a thousand acres of wheat to harvest, cannot reasonably expect to gather it if he be unwilling to employ the number of men indispensably necessary to accomplish it. The moral harvest ripening in the world-field will not gather itself; it cannot be gathered without an adequate number of laborers; and, hence, if the Lord of the harvest has failed to call them, as the theory we are combating presupposes, he cannot expect that it shall be gath-

ered. But the Lord of the harvest does expect that it shall be gathered, imposes the obligation upon the Church to do all that is necessary to save it, and reveals the period when it will have been accomplished. But if the theory under consideration were true, that an inadequate number of men are called into the ministry, then the duty imposed upon the Church to preach the Gospel to every creature, cannot be performed, and, humanly speaking, the kingdoms of this world can never become the kingdoms of the Lord and his Christ.

2. Because it is inconsistent with the adequacy of all the other provisions of redemption. Man is guilty, and needs pardon. Provision is made to secure it through the atonement of Christ, who, by tasting death for every man, became the propitiation for the sins of the whole world. Man is depraved, and needs the sanctification of his nature. Redemption makes provision for this, through the transforming power of the Holy Spirit, whom God has poured out upon all flesh, and promised to give to every one that asketh him. To reveal to man the atonement, and to regenerate his heart, the Gospel is indispensable ; and God has commanded his ministers to preach it to every creature, and given the assurance that it would prove the wisdom and power of God unto salvation. But as the Christian ministry constitutes an essential part of the provisions of redemption, and as all the provisions just mentioned are characterized by universality, that pertaining to the ministry must correspond with them in this respect, involving the call of an adequate number of ministers to proclaim the Gospel to all nations.

3. Because it limits all the provisions of redemption by the measure of the inadequate part. The strength of a chain, capable of raising a thousand pounds, is limited by a single link adequate to bear only a hundred pounds. An adequate supply of medicinal remedies is limited, in its saving efficacy, by the number of physicians engaged in applying it to the diseased. In like manner, will the adequacy of all the essential provisions of redemption be limited by the degree of inadequacy attaching to the deficient part. Just in proportion, therefore, as the number of those called to the ministry is reduced, and rendered inadequate to make Christ and his salvation known to all men, in

that proportion are all the associated provisions of redemption, the atonement, the influence of the Spirit, and quickening power of the Gospel, limited in their saving efficacy. But as such a deficiency in the number of the ministers called, and the consequent limitation of the provisions of redemption, involves the perfection of the plan of salvation, the consistency of its parts, as well as the wisdom and mercy of God, it cannot possibly be true.

4. Because it throws the responsibility of the inadequacy of the number of the ministry and consequent loss of the harvest upon the Lord of glory. The value of a single soul transcends all human calculation. Its ruin constitutes the greatest calamity of the moral universe—its salvation, the greatest achievement of redemption. An adequate number of ministers is indispensable to save the moral harvest; and if the Lord of the harvest be unwilling to call them to the work of gathering it, and in consequence thereof any portion of it perish, it is impossible to discern how the responsibility of such loss can be removed from him. But as his perfection forbids such a supposition and as he himself challenges the universe to lay the responsibility of the loss of mankind upon him, by the interrogatory: "What could I have done unto my vineyard, that I have not done unto it?" the theory that involves it must be false.

5. Because it is unscriptural. An induction, in order to establish its truthfulness, must include all the facts pertaining to it; and just in proportion as the number of facts increases that cannot be interpreted by it, will the probabilities be strengthened that it is not founded upon a scientific basis. An hypothesis that can produce no facts to sustain it, is utterly false. And the same tests must be called into requisition in determining religious questions. Let us apply them to the theory under consideration. Not a single example can be cited from the Scriptures where a person presented himself, either to the apostles, or to a congregation, as one called by the Lord of the harvest, as a laborer (minister), on the ground that he possessed the natural and spiritual qualifications fitting him for the work, and that he had been brought to this conclusion by an internal call

from the Holy Spirit. Nor can a case be adduced where such an applicant was accredited by the apostles, and accepted or chosen by any Christian congregation. The case of Isaiah (vi. 8), who, in answer to the questions put to him by the Lord of glory, "Whom shall we send?—and who will go for us?" said: "Here am I, send me," is ruled out by the fact that he was not on this wise called to the prophetic office, but to some special work as an accredited messenger of God; and the declaration of the Son to the Father, "Lo I come, in the volume of the Book it is written of me, to do thy will, O God!" cannot be legitimately appropriated in bolstering up such pretensions. Although the head and exemplar of the ministry, and although conscious, even from his childhood, that he was called by the Father to be the Prophet of God, like unto Moses, and the Minister of the New Covenant, yet did he not assume this office until he was designated as such by the baptism of John, the visible descent of the Holy Spirit, and the audible voice of God, "This is my beloved Son, in whom I am well pleased." A theory left unsupported by a single relevant example must be purely hypothetical, and prove both delusive and inadequate to supply the Church with a sufficient number of well qualified and duly called and accredited ministers of Christ.

6. Because the scripture passages and precedents appealed to to sustain it are misunderstood and misinterpreted. Moses and the prophets were directly called by God, and the apostles and evangelists by Christ in a similar manner. They were inspired by the Holy Ghost, endowed with the gift of tongues, and invested with miraculous powers, as attestations of their divine appointment. But the immediate call of prophets ceased with Malachi, and that of apostles, with Paul, and ministers are now called into the sacred office, mediately through the Church. The extraordinary influences of the Holy Spirit, involving direct inspiration, and the power to perform miracles, have also ceased, and all revelations of the divine will, and all communications of religious truth, are now made through the written word, and the ordinary influences of the Holy Spirit, involving a conviction of a call to the ministry, a knowledge of having passed from death unto life, and spiritual assistance in the exer-

cise of prayer and preaching the Gospel. The Anabaptists and other enthusiasts that arose in the Reformation, perverted the passages and precedents of Scripture, referring to the immediate call of prophets and apostles, and their inspiration, and claimed that they were called to the ministry in the same manner, and endowed with the extraordinary influences of the Holy Spirit, superceding the necessity of education, premeditation and study, in prayer and preaching. The following quotations from Luther and Melanchthon, exhibit the fanatical pretensions of these "heavenly prophets" as they were styled in derision.

Melanchthon on the Zwickau fanatics to the elector of Saxony: "I have heard them. It is wonderful what they proclaim concerning themselves, viz, that they have been sent to teach by the clear voice of God, that they have had familiar conversations with God, that they see future things; briefly, that they are prophetical and apostolic men. How I am moved by this, I cannot easily say. For important reasons, I am inclined not to despise them; for that some spiritual beings [*quosdam spiritus*] are in them, is apparent by many proofs, but no one can readily judge thereof except Martin." Concerning this matter Luther writes to Melanchthon: "I do not approve of your timidity, since you excel me both in spirit and learning. In the first place, when they give testimony concerning themselves they are not to be at once heard, but, according to the advice of St. John, the spirits are to be proved. You have, too, the advice of Gamaliel to differ; for so far nothing has been said or done by them which I have heard, that Satan cannot do or imitate. Do you then for me, try if they can prove their call. For God never has sent any one, unless called by man, or with his call attested by signs—not even his own Son. Formerly the prophets derived their authority from the prophetical law and order, just as we now through men. I am entirely opposed to their reception, if they proclaim that they have been called by a revelation alone, since God was unwilling to call Samuel except with the authority of Eli attesting it. So far as to the public function of teaching.

Test also their private spirit. Examine whether they have experienced those spiritual sorrows, and divine pains of birth, deaths and hells. If you hear them proclaiming bland, mild, devout and pious things, even though they say they have been carried up to the third heaven, do not approve them. For the sign of the Son of Man is wanting, which is the only test of Christians, and the sure discerner of spirits. Would you know the place, time and mode of divine conversations? Try them, and do not listen even to Jesus when he boasts, unless you first see him crucified."

Concerning a conference between Luther and Melanchthon, Mark Stübner and Cellarius at Wittenberg, Camerarius says:

"Luther very camly heard Mark narrating his claims. When he had ended, Luther thinking there should be no discussion against such absurd and futile pretensions, gave them this advice: They should consider what they were doing. That none of the things that they mentioned were supported by Holy Scripture, and that they were either the invention of curious thoughts, or the insane and pernicious representations of a lying and deceitful spirit. Cellarius, with frantic voice and gestures, stamping the floor with his feet, and striking the table with his hands, exclaimed that it was an outrage for Luther to presume to have any such suspicions concerning a divine man. But Mark said more calmly: 'That you may know, Luther, that I am furnished with the Spirit of God, I will tell you what you are thinking about. It is this: You are beginning to be inclined to believe that my doctrine is true.' Whereupon Luther replied: 'May the Lord rebuke thee, O Satan.' After this, Luther thought he should have no more words with them, and dismissed them.*

The early Puritans and Quakers fell into similar errors, and set up similar pretensions, in regard to the immediate call and direct revelations from the Spirit.

In corroboration of this we present the following quotations: Alt in his "Geschichte des Christlichen Cultus" speaks thus of the views of the English Puritans: "As a rule, there was always one in each congregation, who generally filled the office of principal speaker, nevertheless he was not the preacher appointed

*Seckendorf, I., pp. 192, 193.

by the congregation, but only that member of the same on whom, above others the gift of teaching had been bestowed. And when the Spirit seemed to have departed from him, they, without any hesitation, elected another in his place. For the prevailing of the Gospel was not to be a matter of office and calling, but a work of the Holy Spirit, and the preacher became, in the Old Testament sense of the word, a prophet."

Barclay in his Apology sets forth the theory of the Quakers: "As by the light or gift of God, all true knowledge in things spiritual is received and revealed, so by the same, as it is manifested and received in the heart, by the strength and power thereof, every true minister of the Gospel is ordained, prepared and supplied in the work of the ministry. * * Moreover, they who have this authority may and ought to preach the Gospel, *though without human commission* or literature." Further, Barclay says that this light or gift of God is of such a nature "that these divine revelations are not to be subjected to the test, either of the outward testimony of the Scriptures or the natural reason of man, as to a more noble or certain rule or touchstone; for this divine revelation and inward illumination is that which is evident and clear of itself."*

Although most of those who hold the prevalent theory of a call to the ministry discard the extremes into which the Anabaptists, the English Puritans and the Quakers were led, nevertheless, in so far as they deny that the conviction of a call to the ministry is called forth according to the laws of the human mind, as affected by the truths revealed in the Scriptures, under the ordinary influence of the Holy Spirit, and maintain that it originates in some impulse, impression, or intimation wrought by the direct influence of the Holy Spirit, they occupy substantially the same ground on which all the other extravagant pretensions of the enthusiasts and mystics are predicated.

THE TRUE THEORY STATED.

The constitutional endowments, spiritual gifts, and voluntary exercises, that enter into the constitution of a call to the ministry are the following : Such natural talents as would, if properly

---

*Schwenkfeldt, Böhme, and most of the mystics entertained similar views.

cultivated, qualify the individual for the successful prosecution of the work of the ministry. Such measures of saving faith and divine grace as would render him a "workman that needeth not to be ashamed" in the kingdom of God. Such views of the true object of life, namely, to glorify God by doing good, as to induce him to devote himself to its attainment. Such a conviction that in the ministry he could do the most good to his fellow men, and glorify God in the highest degree, as would bind the conscience, and impose the obligation to choose it as a profession, and induce the formation of a governing purpose to prepare for and enter it. Such a knowledge of the work of the ministry itself, and of the character and service of the church in which he expects to prosecute it, as will render it both interesting and attractive to him, and impel him to persevere in the prosecution of his course of preparation unto the end, notwithstanding the honors and emoluments held out to him by the world, and in spite of any providential obstacles that might stand in his way.

This call is not miraculous but rational, not extraordinary but ordinary, not immediate but mediate. It is not communicated in an arbitrary, but in a natural manner. The conviction of its existence is not found in any notion or impulse, impression or desire, that may have at a certain time originated, been felt, or repeated in some peculiar manner, nor by any special indications of Providence, but brought about according to the natural laws governing the exercises of the mind. Neither is it called forth by any special revelation of some particular truth, nor by any inward voice or immediate assurance given by the Holy Ghost, but through the instructions contained in the Sacred Scriptures, apprehended and received through the ordinary influences of the Spirit of God.

The natural talents and spiritual graces, as constituent elements of the ministerial vocation, are all capable of development. In order that the conviction of a call to the ministry may arise in consciousness, they must be brought into voluntary and consistent exercise—in other words, rationally and spiritually cultivated. They cannot develop themselves. If not brought under the influence of their appropriate means, they

will remain dormant. If neglected, and left to develop themselves spontaneously, without mental culture and religious training, the result would be abnormal, irrational, and fanatical.
Their cultivation cannot, therefore, be safely left to chance, caprice or hap-hazard, but must be accomplished by intelligent
and persevering effort. Take natural talents—how can these
be cultivated without schools, colleges and seminaries? True
piety—how can this be attained without the diligent·use of the
means of grace? The true object of life—how can correct
views concerning it be imparted without special instruction?
The conviction that in the ministry highest usefulness could be
attained and God glorified—how can that be called forth, without an adequate knowledge of its nature, requirements, adaptations and usefulness? The attractiveness of the work and service of the Church which calls him to enter the ranks of her
ministry—how can these be exhibited without portraying the
divine origin, the special mission, and the glorious consumma-
tion, designed to be accomplished by the Church of Christ, and
without an acquaintance with the history, distinguishing characteristics, achievements and field of usefulness offered him by the
Church to whose ministry he proposes to devote his life?

In giving, developing and responding to a call to the ministry, three parties are specially interested—God, the person
called, and the Church. God, through creation, confers the
necessary natural talents; through his Son he redeems the candidate, through the Scriptures commands him to believe in
Christ, to consecrate himself to the service of God, and to glorify him in eating, in drinking, and in all other things; through
the Holy Spirit he works faith, renews and sheds abroad the
love of God and man in the heart, leads him into the kingdom
of God, induces him to choose the ministry, and to devote his
life to winning souls. Through Providence he preserves his
health and life, directs him to suitable fields of labor, and opens
to him doors of usefulness. The Church must call into requisition all the agencies and instrumentalities, and put forth all the
efforts, required to develop the talents and graces conferred,
that it may become manifest to her, that this and that young
man, found in her families, congregations, schools and colleges,

possesses the necessary, natural, spiritual and acquired attainments to qualify him for the ministry and by her counsels, instructions and prayers, render him such assistance as will enable him to form an intelligent judgment that he is called to the ministry. And the candidate must so appreciate the instructions and heed the advice of the Church, as to respond to her call for laborers and enter her service as an ambassador of Christ.

OF THE CHURCH CALLING HER ELECT SONS INTO THE MINISTRY.

God having conferred the natural talents and spiritual gifts adapted to qualify many of the sons of the Church for the office of the ministry, it becomes her bounden duty to call them out and employ them in her service. Among the agencies and institutions through which she is to supply herself with an adequate number of well-qualified ministers, we mention—

1. *The Family.* God instituted marriage, and founded the family as the home of childhood, the guardian of youth, and the nursery of the ministry. In order to attain this exalted end, it is manifest that the family must be constituted according to the Christian ideal. The parents should be intelligent and pious— should consecrate their children to God in holy baptism, that the blessings of the covenant of grace may be sealed unto them —and recognize him at the domestic altar. They should bring them under the 'constant influence of Christian nurture, involving religious instruction, faithful discipline, and a consistent example, that they may become wise unto salvation through faith in Jesus Christ. They should keep constantly before the minds of their children the ultimate end of life, to glorify God, and make well-directed efforts to induce them to devote themselves to its attainment by cultivating excellency of character and doing good. They should give special heed to the constitutional peculiarities, disposition, bent of mind, tastes, or genius, adapting them for some particular trade, profession or business, and give them timely counsel in choosing an honorable and useful calling, as well as afford them the necessary facilities to prepare them to engage in it. They should consider the claims of the ministry as a profession affording opportunities of highest usefulness and possessing corresponding attractions, recog-

nize the probability that one or more of their sons may possess the requisite talents and graces to fit him or them for its prosecution, and endeavor by advice, instruction and assistance, to lead them to devote their lives to the glorious work of saving souls.

2. *The Congregation.* The Christian congregation, as a supernatural organism, is the legitimate outgrowth of the family, and becomes its indispensable auxiliary in calling forth ministers. Provision should, therefore, be made by every congregation to furnish a due proportion of candidates for the ministry. Sunday or parochial schools, or both, should be established, in which the religious training begun in the family may be carried forward in forms adapted to the growth and mental development of youth. Catechetical instruction should be maintained, every pastor diligently prosecute it, and every baptized child brought by parental authority under its moulding and indoctrinating influence. It should be taken for granted that there are some young men in every congregation, who possess the natural and spiritual endowments constituting the marks of a call to the ministry; and Sunday-school teachers and officers, elders and deacons, pastors and church members, should regard it their duty to look after talented, pious young men, call their attention to the claims of the ministry, and in all rational and scriptural ways endeavor to convince them that the Master has need of them, and calls them to labor in his vineyard. The call to and the supply of the ministry should constitute subjects for occasional discussion in the pulpit; regular and liberal contributions should be made to beneficiary education, and the prayer: "Lord, send forth laborers into thy harvest," should find frequent utterance from every Christian lip, in the closet and at the family altar, no less than in meetings for social prayer, and in the supplications of the great congregation engaged in public worship.

3. *The School.* As education consists in cultivating all the intellectual and moral faculties of the soul in due proportion, all schools designed to impart it must adopt such a course of instruction as will be adapted to the attainment of the ultimate end of education, which is character. Every school, whether popular or academic, that discards moral and religious instruc-

tion, cannot be adapted to the training of the sons of the Church, among whom she must look for her candidates for the ministry.

The American system of popular education is acknowledgedly characterized by many excellencies. Its greatest deficiency is found in its want of adequate religious instruction. In a great majority of our public schools the Bible is read, the Lord's Prayer repeated, and a general religious impression made, but it cannot be claimed that this is all the moral instruction needed by the American citizen, and much less than that which the Church should be satisfied to secure for the children she has dedicated to God and covenanted to bring up in the nurture and admonition of the Lord. From many public schools, however, the Bible has been excluded, and no religious instruction whatever is given to the pupils. If this process of divesting our public schools of their religious character should continue, and the American system of popular education become thoroughly secularized, the Church cannot safely patronize them ; and if she cannot redeem and make them Christian, she will be compelled to fall back on the parochial system, and establish not only her own colleges and academies, but also her own parochial schools—as indispensable to the proper education of her sons called to the ministry.

4. *The College.* The course of education commenced in the parochial or common school, and continued in the academy or high school is completed in the college, which becomes one of the most important agencies, not only in giving candidates for the ministry the necessary literary outfit, but also in multiplying their number. Most of their students are distinguished by a thirst for knowledge, and a due appreciation of higher education, and among them a considerable proportion are found possessing the requisite natural talents, which, if properly cultivated and sanctified, would fit them for the work of the ministry. Some of them, although dedicated to the service of God in baptism, have not yet voluntarily confirmed the vows made by their parents in their name. Others, who have already become pious and united with the Church, have not yet chosen a profession in which to prosecute their life work. The college accordingly becomes a nursery, where the sons of the Church, as choice

household plants, are set out, and subjected to the highest mental and moral culture, and among whom the Church must look for the evidences of a call to the ministry and induce them to enter her service.

The establishment of an adequate number of well manned and adequately endowed colleges, becomes a necessity to every Christian denomination ; and upon their religious character, the bearing of their pious students, and the efforts made by their instructors, will depend their efficiency and usefulness in educating and multiplying the number of able and successful ministers of the Gospel. A high standard of piety should be maintained by the professors of religion in colleges, that the students having the ministry in view may be led to carry out their purpose to enter it. Those known as candidates for the holy calling should set such an example of Christian consistency in their walk and conversation, that they may not become a reproach and by-word to the impenitent and a stumbling block to pious students who have not yet decided the question of a profession for life. Ordinary, as well as special efforts should be made by the pastors of college churches, the president and the professors, to bring the non-professing young men under their care to a saving knowledge of Christ. The claims of the ministry as a profession, adapted to the attainment of greatest usefulness, should at all suitable times be presented, and such counsel and instruction given to those exhibiting the natural and spiritual traits, indicative of a call to the ministry, as will enable them to come to an intelligent, conscientious, and satisfactory conclusion, that it is their duty to become ministers of the Gospel.

5. *The Pulpit.* The pulpit is made to stand by metonymy for the preacher, the sermon and everything else pertaining to the ministry. As pastors of congregations and representatives of the whole Church, they are charged with the duty of giving succession to the ministry, which requires careful observation, sound judgment, and the application of necessary tests. The natural and spiritual qualifications for which they must look, as manifest indications of a call to the ministry, are specifically set forth in the Scriptures ; and it is expressly enjoined upon them to exercise proper caution, subject to adequate trials, and guard

against undue haste in committing the ministerial office, "by the laying on of hands," to their successors. Ministers should take a deep interest in the lambs of the flock, notice children in their visitations, keep an eye on the boys in school and young men in college ; and those, in whom they discover the natural and spiritual qualifications adapted to the prosecution of the work, they should endeavor to convince that they are called to the office of the ministry. They should place a due estimate upon the ministerial profession, make themselves thoroughly acquainted with, and inculcate correct views concerning it in their conversations, ministrations and writings.

The indirect influence of the pulpit in calling forth ministers is no less important. As the sons of the Church, elect of God, are to be nurtured in the family, trained in the congregation, and educated in the school and the college, and as the manifestations of the marks, as well as the number and character of the ministry, depend upon the efficiency of religious training and Christian education, it follows that just in proportion as pastors labor to promote Christian nurture in the family, to elevate the standard of intelligence and piety in the congregation, and to improve moral and religious instruction imparted in popular and parochial schools, academies and colleges, in that proportion will the number and character of candidates for the ministry be increased and elevated. No greater service than this can the pulpit render to the Church, and the low estimate placed upon the ministry, and its consequent general neglect, must be set down among the principal causes that have led to the paucity and inefficiency of ministers.

6. *The Press.* The press is the most important of modern inventions in stimulating, preserving, and communicating knowledge, and the Church has wisely availed herself of its almost omnipresent influence in every department of her work. She has accordingly provided herself with a religious literature, priceless in value, and all-permeating and powerful in its influence. In the form of books, she has treasured up and disseminated a permanent and sanctified literature, and through her periodicals she has supplemented and greatly widened the sphere

of her influence; and the bearing of both forms of religious literature upon the increase of the number and the elevation of the character of the ministry, is very great. Distinct treatises on the ministry, the symbolical writings of her confessors, the works of her theologians, the discourses of her great preachers, the achievements of her pastors and churches recorded by her historians, and the commentaries of her expositors, are all calculated to set forth the nature, character, qualifications, usefulness, and claims of the ministry, and to exert a corresponding influence on all Christians interested in and obligated to take part in calling forth candidates, and in advancing the standard of ministerial qualifications.

The weekly church paper, originated in America, and scarcely three-quarters of a century old, has not only become an indispensable means of spreading religious intelligence, cultivating personal piety, fostering the spirit of liberality, and stimulating Christian activity in every department of church work, but has also proven the most efficient auxiliary to the agencies heretofore mentioned in calling the attention of the churches to the deficiency in the ministry, and in urging the duty of making intelligent and constant effort to increase their number and improve their character and efficiency. These important results are attained by the church paper, through the publication of articles on the call and other aspects of the ministry, reports of the contributions made and the number of beneficiaries supported by our synods, the number of theological students sustained by their parents, the proportion among the young men in our preparatory schools and colleges having the ministry in view, the notices of licensures and ordinations taking place at our synodical meetings, the destitution in our own and the still greater destitution in foreign lands, the calls of our missionary boards and their secretaries for more men, accounts of missionary meetings at synods and conventions, reports of home and foreign missionaries, as well as references to the writings of ministers, and their addresses and sermons on special occasions, the labors of pastors and missionaries at home and abroad, with the additions made to their congregations, reports of revivals of religion, in which scores and even hundreds are brought to the knowledge of the truth and gathered into the kingdom of God, together with such other articles bearing more or less directly on the ministry, and such other items of Church intelligence, as are calculated to foster church love, religious enterprise, and Christian benevolence, and referring more or less directly to the subject and claims of the ministry. On this wise, the church paper sounds the call of Jesus addressed to talented and pious young men : "Son, go work to-day in my vineyard." It becomes an assistant to parents in the family and to pastors in the congregation, and a co-worker with the teacher in the school and the professor in the college, in calling forth and educating an adequate number of able ministers to preach the gospel to every creature, and convert the world to Jesus Christ, who is "head over all things to the church," "God blessed forever."

The truth of this theory may be argued:

1. *From Scriptural Analogy.* The ordinary call to accept the Gospel embraces the general call, to believe in Christ, and to go into his vineyard and work, as well as the special call to perform such a part of the work required as each one was specially fitted for. In this manner members of the church at Jerusalem received and responded to the general gospel call, but when the special work of distributing alms was required, a certain number of them received a specific call to attend to it, the qualifications required were pointed out by the apostles, the Church directed to choose them, and when thus chosen the apostles set them apart to their work. In this manner the office of deacon was instituted and the call to the deaconship developed by the Church. A special service of a similar character was called for among the women, then secluded from the ordinary society of men. Certain qualifications were required, those possessing them were regarded as called to engage in it, and the Church appointed them. Thus the office of deaconesses arose and pious women were called to fill it.

2. *From Scriptural Precedent.* The informing or governing idea of the call to the ministry, viz, that of special fitness for the performance of its duties, runs through the procedure of God in calling Christ, of Christ in calling the evangelists and the apostles, and of the apostles in calling pastors, and other officers

to the performance of specific services in the Church. God, the Father, having determined to redeem the world, needed a Redeemer. Finding the qualifications necessary to accomplish it in his Son, he called him to the work of redemption, and when he communicated the call to him, the Son responded: "Lo, I come, in the volume of the book it is written of me to do thy will, O God!" And he accordingly expressly declared to the Jews, "I came not of myself, but the Father sent me."

A special service became necessary, viz, to make known and to prepare the way for the coming of Christ to certain places in Palestine. The Saviour apprehended the qualifications required to perform it, and finding them in the seventy disciples, he sent them forth as his evangelists.

Witnesses of his resurrection, and mediums of divine revelation, were necessary to establish the Christian Church. In the twelve apostles and in Paul, Jesus discovered the requisite qualifications, in consequence of which he called them to the work of the apostleship.

As Jesus had called evangelists and apostles, so, too, did he authorize the apostles to call pastors, evangelists, teachers, prophets, "for the perfecting of the saints and the edifying of the body of Christ." And those in whom they found the necessary qualifications, through their own observation, inquiry among the members of the churches, or otherwise, they regarded as called of God to perform such parts of the work required as they were severally best fitted for, and through their own agency and the coöperation of the churches, they convinced those called of their duty, and induced them to devote themselves to the offices above designated.

3. *From the Analogy of Faith.* The truthfulness of any theory propounded in the domain of science can only be demonstrated by showing that all the facts pertaining to the subject accord with it. Newton, having conceived the theory of gravitation, viz, that the force of gravitation operates directly as the quantity, and inversely as the square of the distance, demonstrated its truth by showing that the movements of all the planets and their satellites accorded with it. In other words, when the subjective idea and the objective law correlate a theory is

demonstrated. The truth of the theory under consideration may be tested in the same manner. In order to demonstrate it, all the passages bearing on the call to the ministry must be collated, and interpreted by the theory, and if such interpretation accords with the principles of hermeneutics, the demonstration becomes complete, and theological truth is established.

Having subjected our theory to a partial induction, embracing scripture analogy and precedent, we now extend it to all other passages of Scripture having reference to it, and render it all comprehensive. We herewith give a number of them:

"No man taketh this honor unto himself, but he that is called as was Aaron," Heb. 5 : 4. A bishop then must not be a novice, apt to teach, a workman that needeth not be ashamed, rightly dividing the word of truth. They must also first be proved and have a good report from them that are without. (See 1 Tim. 3d c.) "But when it pleased God, who separated me from my mother's womb, and called me by his grace to reveal his Son in me, that I might preach him among the heathen; immediately I conferred not with flesh and blood," Gal. 1 : 15, 16. "Neglect not the gift that is in thee, which was given thee by prophecy, with the laying on of the hands of the presbytery," 1 Tim. 4 : 14. "Necessity is laid upon me, yea, woe is unto me, if I preach not the Gospel," 1 Cor. 9 : 16. "Lay hands suddenly on no man," 1 Tim. 3 : 22. "The things that thou hast heard of me among many witnesses, the same commit thou to faithful men, who shall be able to teach others also," 2 Tim. 2 : 2. "For this cause left I thee in Crete, that thou shouldst set in order the things that are wanting, and ordain elders in every city, as I had appointed thee," Titus 1 : 5. "And when they (i. e. Paul and Barnabas) had ordained them elders in every church, and had prayed with fasting, they commended them to the Lord, on whom they believed," Acts 14 : 23.

From a careful examination of these passages, each class of which could have been considerably enlarged, the following points are clearly and consistently set forth : That no man has a right to take unto himself the office of the ministry at his own option or choice ; that those designed to preach the Gospel

must be called of God; that this call is not now given by him
immediately, but mediately, through the Church, that is through
her members or pastors; the qualifications, natural and spiritual
for which the representatives of the Church must look and by
which they are to be governed in their judgment and choice,
are explicitly and fully set forth in the Scriptures; that both
their qualifications and character must be proved, by the appli-
cations of the texts just referred to, not only before the eyes of
the Church, but also of the world; that a number of constitutional and intellectual deficiencies and defects of character are
also stated in the Scriptures, as constituting marks of unfitness
for the ministry, and from the exhibitions of which, in any
given case, they were to draw the conclusion, that such persons
were not called to the ministerial office; that in accordance
with these instructions, they should take adequate time in de-
ciding every individual case, and lay hands suddenly on no man;
that when all these requisitions had been fully complied with,
then, and then only, were they authorized to commit the office
of the ministry to such as proved themselves to be "faithful
men," and worthy to be ambassadors of Jesus Christ; and that
Paul and Barnabas, Timotheus and Titus, acted according to
these directions, in selecting pastors for the congregations then
organized, and by their instructions and example, settled the
Scriptural theory of a call to the ministry, by which alone her
elect sons can be called out, educated and ordained in sufficient
numbers, not to supply her own pulpits, but to make known
the glad tidings of salvation among all nations. It is hardly
necessary to remind the reader that all the points just presented
accord with the scripture precedents and examples heretofore
set forth, and render our argument from the analogy of faith
complete and conclusive. An attempt to make all this accord
with the prevalent theory of a call to the ministry, might, indeed, be made, and by artfully mixing up references to examples of the extraordinary call like that of Paul cited above,
through the direct influences of the Holy Ghost, with the ordinary call, mediately communicated by the Church, and developed by the ordinary influences of the Spirit through the truth,
but such a course perverts the testimony of the Scriptures, con-

founds calls that are distinct, is illogical, and can never be established, and successfully carried out, as the present threatened
famine in the ministry abundantly proves.

4. *From the Universality of the Priesthood of Believers.*
In the Mosaic economy, the priesthood was confined to the
tribe of Levi, and the high priesthood to the family of Aaron,
and transmitted by natural descent, constituting an hereditary,
sacerdotal order.   The Romish Church modeled its priesthood
after the Levitical pattern, constituting an indelible priesthood,
or clerical order, according to which he who is "once a priest"
remains "always a priest."   Luther, under the guidance of the
New Testament, held that all hereditary restrictions in the priesthood had been abrogated with the Jewish dispensation to which
it belonged, and maintained that in the Christian economy all
believers became priests.   The positions taken by him, and the
arguments by which he sustained them, are so characteristic
and conclusive that we subjoin a translation of the principal
parts thereof:

*All Christians are priests through Christ; the preachers have
only an ecclesiastical office.*   Christ is priest, therefore all Christians are priests; that this is a true and Christian inference is
evident from Psalm 22 : 22: "I will declare thy name unto my
brethren," and again Ps. 45 : 7, "Therefore, God, thy God, hath
anointed thee with the oil of gladness above thy fellows."
That we are his brethren is effected alone through the new
birth ; therefore, we are also priests as he is, we are sons as he
is, kings as he is.   For he has "raised us up together and made
us sit together in heavenly places," that "we should be made
heirs" and that God should "with him also freely give us all
things."   Eph. 2 : 6, Tit. 3 : 7, Rom. 8 : 32.   And we have be-
sides also many similar scripture passages in which we are identi-
fied with Christ, as one bread, one drink, one body, one member
with another, one flesh, bone of his bones ; yes, that we have all
things in common with him.

But let us proceed and prove also from the offices of the priests
(as they are called) that all Christians are in the same way
priests.   The priestly offices are chiefly the following : teaching,
preaching and proclaiming the word of God, baptizing, blessing

or administering the sacrament of the altar, binding and loosing from sins, praying for others, offering sacrifices, and judging
all other doctrines and spirits.

The first and most important, upon which all the rest depends,
is the teaching of the word of God. For with the word we
teach, bless, bind and loose, baptize, offer sacrifice, judge and decide everything; so that we cannot at all withhold anything
that belongs to a priest from him whom we entrust with the
word. But this same word is the common heritage of all
Christians, as Isaiah says, 54 : 13 : "And all thy children shall
be taught of the Lord." Jer. 6 : 45, Rom. 10 : 17, Ps. 49 : 6
and following.

That the first office, namely, that *in the word of God*, is common to all Christians, is further improved by 1 Peter 2 : 9: "Ye
are a royal priesthood, an holy nation, a peculiar people: that
ye should show forth the praises of him who hath called you
out of darkness into his marvelous light." Who are they, I
beg of you, who are called from darkness into the marvelous
light? Is is not all Christians? But Peter gives them not only
the right but also a command, that they show forth the praises
of God, which surely is nothing else than the preaching of the
word of God. Now let them come along with their two sorts
of priesthood, one spiritual and general, the other special and
external, and pretend that Peter is here speaking of the spiritual priesthood. What is then the office of their special and
external priesthood? Is it not to show forth the praises of God?
But Peter here imposes this duty upon the spiritual and common priesthood.

Christ teaches the same through Matthew, Mark and Luke,
when in instituting the holy supper he says : "This do in remembrance of me." But this remembrance is nothing else than
the preaching of the word; for Paul thus explains it, 1 Cor. 11 :
26: "As often as ye eat of this bread and drink of this cup, ye
do proclaim the Lord's death till he come."

Now, to proclaim the Lord's death is the same as to show
forth the praises of the Lord who has called us from darkness
into his marvelous light. * * St. Paul also confirms the same
truth, 1 Cor. 14 : 26, when he says to the whole Church and to

every individual Christian : "Every one of you hath a psalm, hath a doctrine, hath a tongue, hath a revelation, hath an interpretation." And in verse 31 : "For all may prophesy, one by one, that all may learn and all may be comforted." Now, my dear friend, do tell me what he means when he says *every one ?* What is the meaning of the little word *all ?*

The second office is *baptizing.* They have themselves by daily custom made this general, even allowing women to perform it in cases of necessity.

- The third office is that of *blessing or administering the holy bread and wine.* * * Christ said : "This do in remembrance of me." This he said to all who were present, and to all who thereafter should eat and drink of this bread and wine.   *   * Paul also witnesses to this I Cor. 11 : 23 ; Matt. 6 : 25.

The fourth office is *binding and loosing.* Here comes the word of Christ, Matt. 18 : 15, which he spake not only to the apostles, but to all the brethren. Also verses 17 and 18.

The sixth office is *praying for others.* But Christ gave to each and every one of his Christians a single daily prayer, which, of itself, sufficiently proves and confirms the truth that there is but one priesthood common to all.

The seventh and last office is that of *judging all doctrines.* John 10 : 5 : "My sheep do not hear the voice of strangers." And Matt. 7 : 15 : "Beware of false prophets." Matt. 16 : 6 ; Matt. 22 : 2, 3 ; John 6 : 45.

We are told, Matt. 23 : 8 : "One is your master, even Christ, but ye are all brethren." Therefore we are all equal and we have all only *one* right. For it is not to be at all endured that, among those who are called brethren, and who have all a common inheritance, one should be above another, should receive a larger share and have a better prerogative than another, especially in spiritual matters, of which we are now speaking.

Now, what we have here said has reference only to the common right and power of all Christians. For, although all the things we have mentioned are said to be common to all Christians (as we have indeed shown and proved), yet it is not becoming in any one to put himself forward and appropriate to

himself what belongs to us all. You may assume this right
and exercise it where there is no other one who has received
such a right. But the right of the community demands that
one, or as many as the congregation may please, be chosen and
appointed, who, in the stead and in the name of all the rest who
have the same right, may publicly perform the functions of
these offices, so that there arise no abominable confusion among
the people of God, and that the Church, in which all things
should be done decently and in order, as the apostle teaches, 1
Cor. 14 : 40, be not changed into a Babel. It is one thing for
a man to exercise, by the authority of the congregation, a right
that is common to all, and it is quite another thing for him to
assume for himself to do it in a case of necessity. In a congregation where the right is free to all, no one should assume the
exercise of it without the will and choice of the whole congregation; but in a case of necessity any one who chooses may
avail himself of it.

Now I think it clearly appears from all this that those who
administer the word and sacraments to the people neither can
nor should be called priests. If they are called priests, that is
done either in imitation of the heathen or it is a remnant of the
laws of the Jewish people; hence it has wrought great harm to
the Church. But in accordance with scripture usage they should
rather be called servants, deacons, bishops, stewards, who also
in view of their age are called presbyters, *i. e.* elders; for Paul
says, 1 Cor. 4 : 1, "Let a man so account of us as of the ministers of Christ and stewards of the mysteries of God." (He
did not say—regard us as the priests of Christ; he knew very
well that the name and office of priest was common to all).
Hence comes that familiar word of Paul, *dispensation*, or in
Greek, ὄικονόμια; in German, *haushalten*, [stewardship]; also,
ministerium, minister; in German *dienst* [service]; *amt* [office],
and *diener* [servant].

If then they are merely servants, then there is an end, too, of
the ineradicable mark of their priesthood, and of the perpetuity
of their priestly dignity. That one must always remain a priest
is an invention; on the other hand, a servant can be dismissed
if he prove no longer faithful. But he can be kept in office as

long as he is deserving and is satisfactory to the congregation, just as every one who, among equal brothers, exercises a common office among them in secular affairs.

We have here learned, clearer than the day and more surely than sure, whence we are to take the priests or servants of the word; namely, we are to elect them from the mass of Christ's followers, and nowhere else. For, as it has been sufficiently proved that every one has the right to administer the word, yes, that it is his duty to do so if he sees that either there is no other one at hand to do it, or that those who do are teaching wrongly, as Paul states, I Cor. 14 : 27 sq., so that the praise of God may be shown forth by us all; how much more should not a whole congregation have the right, and this duty too, that by a general election it could commit such an office to one or more in its stead, and set these apart as office-bearers over the others with their consent.

This is what Paul does, 2 Tim. 2 : 2, when he says: "The same commit thou to faithful men, who shall be able to teach others also." Here Paul throws aside all ceremony—cares for no consecration, demands only such as are capable of teaching, and all he wants is that to them alone the word be committed. When thus the office of the word is conferred upon some one, there are conferred with it all the offices that are administered by means of the word in the Church, i. e., the authority to baptize, to bless, to bind and loose, to pray, and to judge or decide. For the office of preaching the Gospel is the highest of all.

Condition. Although every one has authority to preach, yet we should not employ any one to do it, and no one should undertake to do it, unless he be better fitted for it than others. And others should give way to him, so that suitable honor, discipline and order be observed. For thus Paul commands Timothy, 2 Tim. 2 : 2, that he should commit the preaching of the word to those who were fitted for it, and could teach and instruct others. For he who is to preach should have a good voice, a good delivery, a good memory, and other natural gifts. If any one has not these, he will do better to be quiet and let another speak.

The Lutheran Church adopted Luther's doctrine of the uni-

versality of the priesthood, according to which all believers become priests of Christ, and each one is called to perform that
part of the work for which he is peculiarly fitted.

According to this view, the ministry does not constitute a
peculiar order, but an office of special service in the Church, to
which all are called who possess the requisite qualifications to
"labor in word and doctrine." It accordingly becomes the duty
of the Church to look out for the scriptural marks of a call to
the ministry, and endeavor to induce an adequate number of
the universal priesthood to respond to her call to devote themselves to the office of the Christian ministry. Although all
believers are priests, and each one is endowed with the functions of the common priesthood, nevertheless, as all are not endowed with the qualifications necessary to the exercise of the
functions of the ministry, it becomes necessary for the common
priesthood or Church to invest those specially qualified to preach
the Gospel and administer the sacraments, with the prerogatives of the ministry, through ordination conferred by the laying
on of the hands of the presbytery or ministerium, and then to
elect or call them to exercise the office of the ministry as pastors
of their respective congregations, and to commission and send
forth as many others as may be needed to supply the waste
places at home and in foreign lands.

4. *From the Lutheran Doctrine of the Ministry.* This is
stated in the Symbolical Books as follows:

God has appointed the ministry to preach the Gospel and
administer the sacraments. Aug. Conf.

"Concerning Ecclesiastical Orders, they teach that no man
should publicly in the Church, teach, or administer the sacraments, except he be regularly called." A. C., Art. XIV.

"The Church has the command of God to appoint preachers
and deacons. While this is very precious, we know that God
will preach and work through men, and those who have been
elected by man." Apology, Art. IV.

"The churches undoubtedly retain the authority to call, to
elect and to ordain ministers. And this authority is a privilege
which God has given especially to the Church, and it cannot be

taken away from the Church by any human power as Paul testified, Eph. 4 : 8, 11, 12." Smalcald Articles.

Schmid, in his Dogmatic, summarizes the Lutheran doctrine of the ministry as follows: "This office is, therefore, one of divine appointment, and God has, at times, himself called single individuals into it ; while now he does it only mediately, namely, through the Church, which has received from him the right and the authorization to do it." "Individual teachers must now, therefore, have received their call and authorization from the Church, if they are to have legitimately the right to teach and administer the sacraments." We subjoin but a few quotations from those given by Schmid, to sustain the statements quoted above. "By the divine call is understood the appointment of a certain and suitable person to the ministry of the Church, made by God, either alone, or by the intervening judicial aid of men." *Hollaz.*

"God calls men to the ecclesiastical office, sometimes immediately, as Moses and the apostles, and at other times mediately, viz, through the Church, which in the name of God commits this office to certain persons." *Baier.*

"An immediate call is not to be expected in the Church today." *Hollaz.*

"The difference between the mediate and immediate call consists always and only in this, that the former is effected through ordinary, means, divinely appointed for this purpose, but the latter through God himself. The mediate call, therefore, is to be considered no less a divine call—for it is referred to God as its author—it is based upon apostolic authority—and the same promises belong to those thus called." *Gerhard.*

"The less (or minor) principal cause constituting the ministry is the Church, to which the right has been granted by God of electing, ordaining and calling suitable ministers of the divine word—nevertheless with the observance of becoming order in the exercise of this right. Therefore the examination, ordination and inauguration belong to the presbytery, and the consent, vote and approval to the people." *Hollaz.*

From the above quotations, the Lutheran doctrine, concerning the call and office of the ministry, may be summarily set forth as follows : That Jesus Christ, the head of the Church, has conferred the power of calling pastors to preach the Gospel, administer the sacraments and discipline, and ordain ministers, upon the whole Church. Under the proper distribution of the powers, thus conferred, the right to call or elect their own pastor belongs to the laity, and the authority to preach the Gospel, ordain pastors, administer ordinances, and enforce discipline, is ordinarily vested in the ministry.

The "whole Church," is made up of congregations, congregations of families, and families of members. All church members are invested with the same prerogatives, and obligated to discharge the same duties. As each member is interested in the ministry and partakes of the benefits conferred by their labors, so too is each one privileged and bound to take part in looking out for those young men, who give evidence of possessing the natural talents and spiritual graces, which, if cultivated by education and the means of grace, would fit them for the work of the ministry. And as parents, teachers, professors, church officers, and pastors, are brought into frequent and intimate contact with boys and young men of riper age, it becomes their special duty, to improve the advantages thus afforded them, and by their counsels and instructions, assist those adapted by nature and grace for usefulness in the church, to come to an intelligent conclusion that they are called to the ministry, and to induce them to prepare themselves to labor in the vineyard of Christ. And having in these and other ways taken part in multiplying the number, and improving the character and efficiency of the ministry, they are permitted to exercise the right of electing pastors to exercise ministerial functions in their respective congregations.

THE PREVALENT THEORY AS SET FORTH BY ITS ADVOCATES.

The distinguishing features of the prevalent theory may be learned from the following quotations :

Dr. H. S. Storrs, in his Lectures on Preaching, in referring to his relinquishment of the study of the law, and his entry upon that of theology, says : "When my plans of life were changed, under the impulse, as I thought, of God's Spirit, and I had devoted myself to the ministry, I determined to fit myself for it, and to preach without reading."

Dr. T. D. Witherspoon, in referring to Saul's preaching Christ, says: "The call of Saul of Tarsus was in many respects extraordinary. * * But though the call was thus in its method extraordinary, in essence it was the same that every one must have who would enter upon this office. There must be an impression deeply wrought in the heart by the Spirit of God, that it is our duty to serve him in the ministry, that thus we can best honor him and best fulfil the mission he has given us in the world—a conviction that grows stronger as it is prayerfully deliberated upon and does not yield in prospect of the self-denials and sacrifices which such a life entails."

Bridges, in his Christian Ministry, describes the ministerial call, as follows: "The internal call is the voice and power of the Holy Ghost, directing the will and the judgment and conveying personal qualifications. * *· An inward movement by the Holy Ghost must imply his influence upon the heart, not indeed manifested by any enthusiastic impulse, but enlightening the heart under a deep impression of the worth of souls; constraining the soul by the love of Christ to spend and be spent for him; and directing the conscience to a sober, searching, self-inquiry; to a daily study of the Word; to fervent prayer in reference to this great matter; and to a careful observation of the providential indications of our Master's will."

Bishop Simpson, in his Lectures on Preaching, sets forth his views in the following explicit and discriminating manner: "The first evidence of a divine call is in the consciousness of the individual, and is a persuasion which, slight as it may be at first, deepens into an intense conviction that he is called of God to preach the Gospel." * * "In its slightest form it (the call) is a persuasion that he who receives it *ought* to preach the Gospel; in its strongest form, that God requires him to do this work at the peril of his soul." * * "It is God's voice to the human conscience saying, 'You ought to preach.'" "Admitting the existence of this conviction, how is it known to be of divine origin." * * "I think there is nothing unphilosophical in referring it to a purely spiritual source, even to God him-

self." "In this respect it resembles the work of conversion."
"Peace springs up in the heart, but whence that peace comes,
consciousness alone cannot tell." "Yet the true Christian at
once and correctly ascribes it to a divine source." * * "That
a young man may be truly called of God, but it is impossible
for him to know it, except by way of inference from surrounding indications." "This philosophy I believe to be radically
defective." "Admitting, however, that this knowledge is not
absolute, but merely strongly presumptive, there are other indications which are confirmative." "We are commanded to try
the spirits, whether they be of God, and we have tests by which
the trial can be made." * * "That which is discovered by
one, soon becomes manifest to all, and the Church, in whatever
way it may operate, opens for him a door-way leading into the
ministry." "This call of the Church added to the conscious
call, greatly strengthens the conviction of duty."

"Some writers * * distinguish between what they term the
ordinary and extraordinary call." "In the ordinary call they
teach that the young man arrives at the conviction that he
should preach, from consideration of his qualifications, mental
tendencies and surrounding circumstances; that the same influences lead him to enter the ministry, which, with some changes
would have led him to enter the profession of medicine or law,
or to have engaged in some secular pursuit." * * "So he
selects the ministry believing that thereby he can best promote
his own happiness and the welfare of humanity."

From a careful examination of the quotations just given, the
following points become manifest, and deserve special notice.
The phraseology employed in describing the call to the ministry varies, is somewhat vague, and leaves an ambiguous impression on the mind of the reader. No attempt is made
to explain intelligently the manner and the means through
which the person obtained the knowledge and assurance of the
fact that God designed him for the ministry. One of these
writers says that the Holy Spirit communicates a knowledge of
this call by awakening an *impulse*, another that he accomplishes
it by an *impression*, and a third, that he does it by calling forth

a *persuasion*, each of which culminates in a conclusion, that it is his duty to devote himself to the preaching of the Gospel.

Webster defines the meaning and explains the manner in which impulses, impressions and persuasions produce conviction and oblige the conscience, as follows: Impulse, he represents as "a supposed, supernatural influence or motive on the mind." Impression he illustrates thus: "the truths of the Gospel make an impression on the mind." Persuasion, he defines as "arguments or reasons that move the will to determination." Conviction he declares to be "a strong belief or settled opinion, on the ground of satisfactory evidence." These definitions and explanations show, that such impulses, impressions and persuasions, culminating in a conviction of a call to the ministry, can only be produced by the apprehension of such truths contained in the Scriptures, concerning the ministry, as constitute arguments, reasons, or motives, adapted according to the laws of mind, to call it forth in consciousness. And as this rational and scriptural method of communicating the knowledge of a call to the ministry is denied by the advocates of the prevalent theory, there remains no other method, but that of an immediate call of the Holy Spirit, without any medium of communication, which is tantamount to the reception of a direct revelation by inspiration.

In corroboration of the conclusion just drawn, we call attention to the fact, that these writers make no careful discrimination between the direct manner in which Christ made known their call to the apostles, and the apostles to the elders or pastors of the churches, and the indirect manner in which the Holy Spirit now convinces men of their call to the ministry, through the truths pertaining thereto, revealed in the word of God. No passages of Scripture are quoted and no apostolic examples cited in support of the views maintained. And in so far as reference is made to the call of Paul, it is done in such terms as to leave the impression, that every minister in our day is authorized to look for a revelation of his call by the Holy Spirit, as real, immediate and unmistakable as that made by him to Saul of Tarsus, the miraculous circumstances attending it alone excepted.

We are told that this persuasion may at first be very slight in the consciousness of the individual, and that, although it deepens into an intense conviction of his call, it amounts to little more in the end than a strong presumption, which is to be verified by confirmatory tests drawn from the Scriptures. But no such uncertainty attached to the divine call in the Apostolic churches, and this admission of uncertainty as regards the reality of the call in our day, throws the veil of doubt over the sufficiency of the knowledge communicated by the Spirit, and proves that his revelations on this subject have become defective, and cannot now be relied upon with any great degree of certitude.

It is also stated that conscience must impel to the study of the Scriptures, as a confirmation of the inward call, but the Word is not recognized as the instrument of the Spirit in calling it forth. The Church is also mentioned, but her office is represented as that of recognizing and endorsing the judgment of the individual, that he has received a direct call from the Spirit, followed by ordination through her ministers, and subsequently by an election from the laity. But no part is assigned her in calling out those whom she judges to be possessed of the proper natural and spiritual qualifications, to fit them for the office of the ministry.

It is further maintained that a person, in whose consciousness the conviction has arisen, that he is called to the ministry, has the same reason for attributing it to a spiritual source, yea, even to God himself, as the Christian has for believing that the peace which sprang up in his heart at the time of his conversion, was imparted to him by the direct witness of the Spirit. But as the Father bears witness to his existence and attributes through the effects produced in nature, and the Son bore witness to his messiahship through his works, so, does the Spirit bear witness with our spirits, that we are the children of God, through the effects produced on our minds and hearts ; in other words, through the work and fruits of the Spirit, as described in the Scriptures, and not by any new and direct revelation made to the soul. And the manner in which the Spirit bears witness of a call to the ministry, is the same, viz., through the truths revealed by him in the word of God.

The prevalent theory, as thus explained by its advocates, lies open to the following objections :

1. It constitutes the individual himself the sole judge of his call to the ministry. He has in some mysterious manner become convinced that he is called to the ministry, and he believes that the fact has been communicated to him by the Holy Spirit. He feels bound by conscience to devote himself to the work of preaching the Gospel. He communicates the intelligence either to his parents, pastor or the education committee, who are expected to accept his judgment and recognize the validity of his call.

2. The age, circumstances and manner in which it is claimed that the knowledge of the call was communicated to the individual, invest it with doubt and uncertainty. It takes place usually at an early age, before his natural talents have been developed by education, and his moral character has been fully tested. He has little or no knowledge of the work and requirements of the ministry, nor of his adaptation, through his natural and spiritual gifts, for its successful prosecution. Neither has he any intelligent apprehension of the means and manner in which the Holy Spirit now begets a conviction of a call to the ministry, but takes it for granted that he received his impressions immediately from the Holy Spirit. A youth of tender age, immature in mind, without a proper knowledge either of himself, the workings of the Spirit or the ministry, without experience and without counsel, decides that God designed him for the ministry, and, as might well be anticipated, mistakes his calling, and proves a failure.

3. No satisfactory evidences are furnished, and no adequate tests can be applied to verify this immediate call. The ministry is the highest of all professions, and imposes the greatest responsibilities. It involves not only the character, usefulness and destiny of the incumbent, but also the interests and salvation of men. No man has a right to assume it without satisfactory evidence, and no one should be invested with it without having been "proved" according to the Scriptures. But such is the nature and source of this call, that it rests upon no other evidence than the testimony of the individual that the Holy

Spirit has revealed to him the fact. No satisfactory proofs can be furnished to substantiate it, and all the tests furnished by the Scriptures as safeguards against the introduction of novices, blind guides, and false prophets into the sacred office, are shut out. Christ himself did not ask men to accredit him as a messenger from God, without appealing to the witness of his character and works; and a theory of the ministerial call that excludes spiritual credentials and scriptural tests, cannot be the true one.

4. The Anabaptists and other enthusiasts of the Reformation period, as well as other religious pretenders in both ancient and modern times, have set up the claim that they had a direct call from the Holy Spirit, that he indited their utterances, and that they had received immediate revelations. While most of the advocates of the prevalent theory would repudiate such extreme pretensions, and some of those mentioned above have uttered express disclaimers against such delusions, it nevertheless remains true that the language they employ in setting forth their views makes the same impression. And their disclaimers, although designed to guard against such an interpretation, simply reveal their inconsistency, and constitute a corroboration of the true theory, extorted from them by the manifest absurdity of such pretentious claims.

5. A man's entrance upon the ministry, according to the prevalent theory, becomes an exception to his selection of any other calling in life, whether secular or ecclesiastical. The selection of some vocation becomes indispensable to all men. In making the choice, the person's adaptations, qualifications and preference must be taken into due consideration. The counsel of parents and the advice of judicious friends are in most cases sought in coming to a final decision. In employing men in any department of business, or in electing them to any office of public trust, their characters and qualifications become the controlling considerations in making the engagement on electing the incumbent. Nor is a different course pursued in ecclesiastical affairs. Any officers that were needed were selected on the ground of their fitness to discharge the duties of the special service called for. Now the theory that lays all these prece-

dents aside, and encourages men to choose the ministry, without taking their natural and spiritual qualifications into consideration as the basis of a just decision—without the judgment of any of the representatives of the Church, through a direct call of the Holy Spirit, is not only at variance with the uniform practice in both secular and religious affairs, but also inconsistent with Scripture precedent and apostolic example.

Nor can we overlook another still more glaring inconsistency into which these writers have fallen. While they object to the rational, logical and scriptural method, according to which the Holy Spirit, by means of the truth, enables an individual to draw the legitimate conclusion, that it is his bounden duty to preach the Gospel, they, nevertheless, admit that the source whence the impulse, impression or persuasion has arisen in the consciousness of a person, is unknown to him, and accept his conclusions, that it must have come from the Holy Spirit, yea, from God himself; and that it must mean that he is called to the ministry, on the *ipse dixit* of the individual, without any reference to his natural or spiritual qualifications, or the application, at the time, of any scriptural tests whatever, as a verification of his inferences, and the validity of his convictions of duty. In other words, they reject the legitimacy of the conclusions, logically drawn from premises furnished by nature, grace and Scripture, and rely upon those drawn from the imagination of the individual himself, unsustained by any other proof.

Further, when God, the Father, testifies that a man is not called to the ministry, by creating him, without those constitutional endowments of mind, heart and speech, indispensable to the successful prosecution of the work of the ministry, it is preposterous to suppose that the Holy Spirit, who knows the mind of God, the Father, to contradict his testimony by bearing witness directly to the same individual, that God has called him to the ministry. And yet the simple statement of an individual, that he has received a call from the Spirit, is credited by the advocates of the prevalent theory, in spite of the notorious fact, that in many cases, such pretensions are unsupported by the testimony of the Spirit, given in the Scriptures, setting forth the qualifications that those whom he has called must possess, and contradicted by the testimony of God, the Father, as manifested by the deficiency of constitutional endowments.

THE TRUE THEORY EXPLAINED.

The faculties of the soul brought into operation in imparting the knowledge, and producing the conviction of a call to the ministry are the understanding, the heart, the conscience and the will. Through attention, the understanding apprehends truth and accumulates knowledge; through knowledge, thus obtained, the heart is moved and puts forth emotions; through the knowledge and feelings thus excited, the conscience is acted upon by moral considerations and imposes a sense of obligation, and through the combined operation of truth apprehended, desires awakened, and convictions of duty realized, as motive forces, the will is impelled, to form determinations, culminating in corresponding action. These faculties as conferred in creation, cannot in their natural state, by any form or degree of cultivation, develop a true call to the ministry. In order that this may be effected, it becomes indispensable, that these natural faculties be transformed into spiritual graces. This is accomplished by the Holy Spirit through the means of grace, whereby the natural man is begotten of the truth, born of the Spirit, and made a new creature in Christ Jesus. As in producing conviction of sin the Spirit uses the law and in working faith and regenerating the heart, he reveals the things of Christ, in calling forth the conviction of a call to the ministry, he brings into requisition all the truths of Scripture bearing upon the subject. Through this spiritual transformation, the understanding becomes enlightened, the love of God and of man is shed abroad in the heart, the conscience becomes sensitive to moral impressions, a clear conviction of duty ensues, and the high resolve is formed to devote life to the service of God, in the work of the ministry. Correct views are entertained of the glory of God as the ultimate end of life, a deep and abiding interest is felt in the spiritual welfare of man, a conclusion legitimately drawn, that in the ministry, the greatest usefulness could be attained, and a governing purpose formed, so deep and com-

prehensive, as to effect a permanent change in the radical disposition, and rendering the candidate and the minister suscep-
tible to, and interested in, all ethical and religious subjects and
ecclesiastical affairs.

The following passages may be quoted as having a direct
bearing on the call to the ministry: "Ye are not your own, for
we are bought with a price, therefore glorify God in your body
and in your spirit, which are God's." "Whether therefore ye eat
or drink, or whatsoever ye do, do all to the glory of God."
"Diligent in business, fervent in spirit, serving the Lord." "Son,
go work to-day in my vineyard." "Go thou and preach the
kingdom of God." The parable of the ten talents; the passages describing the qualifications, duties and promises made to
ministers; the directions given by Paul to Timothy and Titus,
embracing the tests they were to apply in determining the question of a call to the ministry: the examples furnished, illustrat-
ing the truths contained in the passages quoted and referred to
together with all the warning against rushing into the ministry
unbidden, and all the threatenings declared against hypocrites
and false teachers, to whom, as "wandering stars, is reserved the
blackness of darkness forever."

Now, as the holy Scriptures contain the whole revealed will
of God, and as such are able to make us wise unto salvation;"
as all men are warned against "being wise above what is written," as it is enjoined upon all to go "to the law and the
testimony" of God for information on all subjects pertaining to
life and godliness; as it is declared of those who speak not according to this word, that there is no truth in them, and as all
men are forbidden to add to or take from the word of God, it
follows that all communications now imparted by the Holy
Spirit are made alone through the word of truth. But the doctrine that the Holy Spirit communicates the knowledge of a
call to the ministry to all who are designed for it, by an immediate and special revelation, contradicts the position sustained
by the passages just quoted, and can no more be established
than can the claims of the enthusiasts that they had received a
direct call from the Spirit, and spake under an immediate inspiration conferred upon them by God. The views just ex-

pressed constitute the legitimate outgrowth of the doctrine, held
by the Mystics, and, in some respects, accepted by the advocates
of the prevalent theory of a call to the ministry, namely that the
Holy Spirit now makes communications to the mind and heart
directly, without the written word, and which necessarily ob-
scures the call to the ministry and envelopes it in the mists of
doubt and uncertainty.   In referring to this, Dr. H. E. Jacobs,
in an article on The Lutheran Doctrine of the Ministry, says
[*Evangelical Review*] : "Wherever the former mystical theory
(of the word) is held, the doctrine of the call to the ministry is
obscured.   The individual is turned away from the revealed
word of God, to search within himself for an undefined inner
call.   The candidate must declare, that he has been inwardly
moved by the Holy Ghost to assume the office, whilst but little
importance is attached to any test whereby a true, inner call,
by the Holy Spirit speaking in the outward words may be distinguished from the vagaries of the individual's fancy."

To the Church the "lively oracles of God are given," and she
has become "the pillar and ground of the truth."   On her the
Holy Spirit has been conferred and the authority given to appoint and commission Christian ministers to preach the Gospel,
and administer the Sacraments.   Through the word preached,
and the Spirit accompanying it, the different truths bearing on
the call to the ministry are disseminated, a correct knowledge
of the subject is obtained, a deep interest is felt in it, and conscience awakens a sense of obligation concerning it, culminating
in a conviction of duty, and moving the will to choose and enter it as a profession for life.

But as the Church is constituted of the ministry and the laity,
and all are commanded to become epistles of truth, the obligation to make known the truths concerning the call to the ministry, rests not only upon the clergy, but also upon parents,
teachers, church officers and members.   And while preaching
is the principal agency of imparting the necessary instruction
concerning the ministry, the Church is bound to resort to all
other instrumentalities of conveying information about it such
as personal conversation, epistolary correspondence, the religious press, and permanent literature.   As the petition, "Thy

kingdom come," implies and imposes the obligation to do everything necessary to make Christ and his kingdom known in all
the earth, so does the prayer, "Lord send forth laborers into
thy vineyard," involve the duty of using all the means adapted
to induce an adequate number of talented and pious young men
to respond to the call of God to enter the ministry. As the
expectation that the kingdom of God will come, through the
daily repetition of the prayer, "Thy kingdom come," without
the use of means, would be a perversion of its true meaning and
prove abortive; the same may be said of the expectation that
an adequate number of efficient laborers will be called into the
world-field of Christ, by the repetition of the prayer, that God
would call them forth through the direct influence of his Spirit,
without the use of the appropriate means by the Church.

Dr. Phillips Brooks, in his "Lectures on Preaching," empha-
sizes the duty of exercising greater vigilance, on the part of the
Church, in introducing men into the ministry, as follows: "Let
us ask then, first, what sort of man a minister should be? It
would be good for the Church, if it were a more common question: "Partly because the *motives which lead a young man to the
ministry are so personal and spiritual*, partly because of our sense
of the magnitude and privilege of the work, which makes us
fear to be the means of excluding any worthy man from it,
partly because, at present, while the harvest is so plenteous, the
laborers are so very few—for these and other reasons, there is
far too little discrimination in the selection of men who are to
preach, and many men find their way into the preacher's office
who discover only too late that it is not their place."

In corroboration of the views just expressed, we present the
following quotations:

"The certainty of a call to the ministry," says Hollazius, "is
derived, not from a new, peculiar and immediate revelation of
the Holy Spirit, but from mediate revelation contained in holy
Scripture. For Scripture teaches the gift, with which a suitable
minister of the Church should be endowed. It also teaches that
the Church has the power of entrusting the holy ministry to
certain persons. If, therefore, a candidate of theology knows,
for the spirit of man knoweth what is in man, that he has been

divinely furnished with those gifts which holy Scripture requires
in a minister of the Church, and he sees at hand, before his eyes,
a written call from any church, having a right to call, he is certain, without any new and immediate revelation of the Holy
Spirit, of his lawful call to the ministry."

Dr. S. S. Schmucker describes the internal call to the ministry as follows : "The conviction of the individual, that God has
designed him for this office.   This conviction is not at the present day produced in an immediate, extraordinary, or miraculous
manner, as in the case of the ancient apostles and prophets.
The ordinary evidences of a call are, undoubted piety, at least
mediocrity of talent, and a desire, or at least an ultimate willingness to serve God in the ministry, and the coöperation of divine
providence by the removal of all insuperable difficulties."—*Popular Theology.*

Dr. H. Ziegler expresses the following views in his "Pastor :"
"The internal call consists in those personal qualifications, which
are requisite to the faithful discharge of all the duties of the
Christian minister.   It is never immediate or supernatural, but
always mediate and ordinary."

Vinet in his Homiletics, after maintaining that no extraordinary call, through the direct influence of the Spirit, can now be
expected, continues : "Now, as the sensible, direct call from
God is wanting, by what can this be supplied?   In other words,
how may we know that we are called ?   *   *   The call to the
ministry evidences itself, like every other, by natural means
under the direction of the word and Spirit of God."

Rev. John Eades, in exhibiting the process of mind through
which the conviction of a call to the ministry is produced, says:
"All those who are inwardly called of God to the sacred office,
have laid to heart the spiritual necessities of their fellow crea-
tures—are willing, ready and desirous, like their blessed Lord,
to undertake the work ; not from any selfish or worldly motive,
but from a principle of glorifying God in the conversion, edification, and salvation of precious and immortal souls."

Dr. C. P. Krauth, in his Theses on the Ministry, distinguishes
between the mediate and immediate call as follows : "Calling
or vocation is a sacred act, whereby God either immediately by

a direct personal call, or mediately, through the Church, sepa-
rates and appoints, as seems' good to him, certain men to be his
co-workers, and stewards of his mysteries. All legitimate calling is either immediate or mediate. We ought not now to expect the immediate calling, either external, by some miraculous
act of God, or internal, by some new revelation made to the
soul of the person called. But no man should seek the office
of the ministry without a persuasion that it is God's will that
he should do so. The mediate calling, legitimately made, is no
less really divine than the immediate. A legitimate mediate
calling is an act whereby men whose fitness for the work of the
ministry has been tested and proved, are chosen by Christ,
through his Church, to teach the Gospel and administer the
Sacraments."

Dr. L. A. Gotwald, in his Holman Lecture on Church Orders,
says: "As regards the office of the ministry, as well as all other
offices in the Church, these two points from the word of God,
are clear, viz., that the endowments or qualifications, which men
may possess for these respective offices, are the gifts to them of
God, and that these express, both to their possessor, and to
others in the Church around him, that the will of God is, that
he upon whom he has thus bestowed such gifts, should exercise
them also, in the particular office for which he is thus especially
fitted. In other words, the divine endowments of a man for the
ministerial office constitute essentially the divine call also to
that office and the will of God, that a man should be in the
office, is expressed by the peculiar fitness which he gives him
for it."

The manner in which the conviction of a call to the ministry
was called forth by the Church in the case of John Knox and
Calvin, against their own misgivings, illustrates the theory
maintained in this article. John Knox was endowed with such
talents, graces and attainments, that it became manifest to the
Church that he was adapted and called to the work of the ministry. He was accordingly frequently solicited in private by his
brethren to undertake the work of preaching, but "had persist-
ently refused, on the ground that he had no talent or call to
these sacred functions. His friends, however, did not desist

from their purpose, but having consulted with their brethren, came to a resolution without his knowledge, that a call should be publicly given him, in the name of the whole membership, to become one of their ministers. The manner in which this determination was carried out, as stated in McCree's Life of Knox, was as follows:

"Accordingly, on a day fixed for the purpose, Rough preached a sermon on the election of ministers, in which he declared the power which a congregation, however small, had over any one in whom they perceived gifts suited to the office, and how dangerous it was for such a person to reject the call of those who desired instruction. Sermon being concluded, the preacher turned to Knox, who was present, and addressed him in these words: 'Brother you shall not be offended, although I speak unto you that which I have in charge, even from all those that are here present, which is this: In the name of God and of his Son Jesus Christ, and in the name of all that presently call you by my mouth, I charge that you refuse not this holy vocation, but as you desire the glory of God, the increase of Christ's kingdom, the edification of your brethren, and the.comfort of me, whom you understand well enough to be oppressed by the multitude of labors, that you take the public office and charge of preaching, even as you look to avoid God's heavy displeasure, and desire that he shall multiply his grace unto you.'

"Then addressing himself to the congregation, he said: 'Was not this your charge unto me? and do ye not approve this vocation?' They all answered 'It was; and we approve it.' Overwhelmed by this unexpected and solemn charge, Knox, after an ineffectual attempt to address the audience burst into tears, rushed out of the assembly and shut himself up in his chamber. His countenance and behavior from that day till the day that he was compelled to present himself in the public place of preaching, did sufficiently declare the grief and trouble of his heart," &c.

The case of Calvin corresponds, in all the main points, with that of Knox. He was diffident of his abilities, shrunk from assuming the office of the ministry, and preferred to remain a lay worker. But such were the impressions made upon those who attended his instructions, that they were convinced that he was called to the ministry, and he yielded to their judgment rather than his own preferences in entering the ministry.

Calvin at Bourges became a teacher both in private conference with inquirers and by discourses in more public assemblies. "Before a year had elapsed," he says, "all who were desirous of a purer doctrine were in the habit of coming to me though a novice and a tyro, for the purpose of learning."

In engaging in such efforts Calvin seems to have yielded to a constraining sense of duty rather than to have followed the bias of his own inclination. "I always preferred the shade and ease and would have sought some hiding place, but this was not permitted, for all my retreats became like public schools."

Neither of these distinguished men claimed that he was led into the ministry by an inner call, but was rather deterred from assuming it, by a consciousness of their deficiencies, as was the case with Moses, Jeremiah and other prophets, and present striking contrasts to those who insist that they have received an inner, direct call from the Spirit, plead that it was accompanied with such a burning desire to preach the Gospel, as to give them no rest until they resolved to engage in it. Bishop Simpson, in his Yale Lectures, maintains that the hesitancy of Knox and Calvin are shared by all who are truly called of God. "There is not an instance," says he, "in Holy Writ, where a true man was·ever anxious to bear the divine message. He always shrank from it, hesitated and trembled."

The term *prevalent*, by which we·have designated the theory we are combatting, indicates that it has been generally accepted as the true one by the Reformed churches. Bishop Simpson declares that it is the theory of the Universal Church, the correctness of which we question, and over against which, we place the Lutheran theory, as stated in her symbols and maintained by her dogmaticians. The prevalence of the mystical notion of a call to the ministry may be accounted for by the radical tendency among the Puritans in their opposition to Romanism, of running into opposite extremes. Rome so emphasized the "letter" in establishing an outward succession in the ministry, thereby ignoring the operations of the Spirit in the heart of believers, while the Puritans so emphasized the "Spirit" that they relied upon the Holy Ghost to call out the ministry without the use of the "letter" of the word as disseminated by the Church. The Anglican by accepting episcopacy from the Roman Church became at the same time inoculated with its claim of the transmission of ministerial grace by the Spirit, through the laying on of the hands of the bishops. Accordingly every bishop must declare, as a condition of ordination, that he was moved to take this office upon himself by the Holy Spirit.

Inasmuch as the Lutheran Church has accepted Prelacy, not *jure divino*, but *jure humano*, in Sweden, Denmark and Norway, and has been exposed to Puritanic influences in this country, it would not be strange if mystical tendencies should be developed, even among her ministers. The following may serve as examples. Although Dr. Schmucker assures us that an immediate call in an extraordinary manner is not to be expected now, nevertheless, by stating that the call consists in a conviction of the individual that God has designed him for this office, and that he cannot be absolved from the obligation to persevere in his preparation for it except by insuperable obstacles placed in his way by Providence, he seems to contradict himself; and makes a vague, if not a Puritanic impression. Dr. Ziegler also declares that the call to the ministry is not now direct and extraordinary, and yet he admits that there are special cases which on account of some remarkable spiritual manifestations at their conversion, become exceptions to those who have received the mediate call from the Church, through the ordinary means of grace, and refers to Dr. Cannon, who in his Pastoral Theology says: "The internal call may be accompanied with a power of the Holy Spirit, and attended by circumstances and events in the lives and the conversion of some minister of Christ, which when compared to those of the many, who piously engage in the good service, may appear to be extraordinary." But to guard against the perversion of such cases, he adds: "But let it be observed, that whatever is uncommon in these instances does not belong essentially to the internal call of God."

In regard to the interpretation given to any peculiar manifestations, claimed to have been received from the Holy Spirit at the conversion of an individual, viz. that they indicate that he is called to the ministry, it may suffice to remark that they can not safely be accepted as marks of a call for which others are authorized to look, and do not constitute examples by which others ought to be governed. Extraordinary experiences of this kind are the boast of the enthusiasts, and they no more prove the genuineness of the conversion of the subjects of them, than that they establish the claim of a call to the ministry set up by religious pretenders. And as the pretensions of the latter when subjected to the tests presented by the Scriptures, prove to be unfounded, so, too, are the interpretations of the experiences of the former, when weighed in the balances of the word of God, found wanting.

Dr. H. E. Jacobs, heretofore quoted, says: "All our theologians recoginize a true movement of the Holy Spirit on the mind of the individual in leading him, through the study of the outward word, to the conviction that it is his duty to seek the holy office and quotes the testimony of Gerhard, as follows:

"We grant that God, by an inner impulse and inspiration, breathes into some this disposition to undertake the ministry of the Church, without regard to dangers and difficulties to which belongs also that mysterious impulse by which some are drawn to the study of theology.   *   *   And if any one desire to apply, in a proper sense, the name of secret call, to these dispositions, both of which are especially worthy of praise, we do not greatly object. Yet, in the meantime, we give the warning, that in order that the doors be not opened to the disturbances of the Anabaptists or the revelations of the enthusiasts, no one, by reason of this secret call, ought to take upon himself the duties of the ministerial office, unless there be added to it the outward and solemn call of the Church." This inner impulse Gerhard afterward declares not to be the call, but "an accident of the same," and a description of the proper disposition or quality in the persons called.

By designating the operations of the Spirit, in convincing a person, through the Word, that it is his duty to preach the Gospel, by the term call, dividing it into an *internal* and *exter-*

nal call, and representing it as constituted of *divine* and *human* factors, as has been done by writers on this subject, it becomes almost impossible, so to distinguish the ordinary call to the ministry now, from the extraordinary call in apostolic times, as to prevent misapprehension and confusion.

Illustrations of this are found in the following examples. Vinet, heretofore quoted, says: "The word call has, when applied to professions of a temporal order, only a figurative signification. * * But applied to the ministry the word approaches its proper sense. When *conscience commands, and obliges us to discharge* a certain task, we *have that which next to a miracle, merits best the name of a call, and it must be nothing less.*"

Dr. G. Diehl, (Diet Lecture, 1877), remarks: "God, who called the prophets in ways so manifest, and by speech so distinct, as to produce *absolute certainty* in their convictions, does now, in ways less marvelous, and circumstances less imposing, produce a similar conviction in the mind of every man whose ministry heaven has authenticated." * *

The careful reader will observe, that while the advocates of the prevalent theory have employed words and phrases in describing it, that express ideas that accord with the representations made concerning the true theory, and *vice versa*, that some of the words and phrases used by Lutheran theologians, in describing the operations of the Spirit, in begetting a call through the Word, correspond with those employed in setting forth the prevalent or mystical theory. This may be accounted for from several considerations. Striking analogies exist between the two theories. Their respective advocates agree that the agent who imparts the knowledge of a call is the Holy Spirit, that the subject to whom it is communicated is a true believer, a new man in Christ Jesus, and that the form in which it is developed in the consciousness, is that of a conviction, so deep as to bind the conscience and lead to the determination to enter the ministry. The main point of difference between them is whether the Holy Spirit imparts a knowledge of the call directly to the soul, or whether he does it mediately, through the several truths pertaining to the ministry, revealed in the Scriptures, and whether the individual is to determine the question of his call from his

own religious experience, or from self-examination in the light
of the Scriptures, the counsel of relatives and Christian friends,
and the judgment of the ministers and members of the Church.
The subject is a very profound one, involving the manner in
which each aspect of truth revealed in the Scriptures concerning the ministry is adapted to effect the several faculties of the
soul, and call forth in their combined operations such a conviction of duty, through the super-added influence of the Holy
Spirit, as constitutes a call to preach the Gospel, as well as the
manner in which the same Spirit communicated the knowledge
of a call directly to the apostles and other ministers in the apostolic churches. To set this subject forth in a consistent and
scriptural manner, requires the clearest conceptions of every
factor that enters into the subject, the most careful and rigid
discrimination of the influence exerted and the impressions
made by each, and the use of the most terse and forcible terms
in describing them. And as such insight, power and discrimination, and felicity of expression, are not the gift of all writers,
such discrepancies and deficiencies as we have just noticed, must
be looked for in the discussion of all intricate theological points.

But we nevertheless insist that there is no medium ground on
which these opposite theories can be fully harmonized by the
introduction of a third theory, as a cross between the two. The
advocates of the immediate call of the Spirit, according to the
prevalent theory, cannot consistently recognize the Scriptures
as the test of verifying it, while they reject them as the means
of calling it forth ; and the advocates of the indirect call of the
Spirit, through the truth, cannot consistently admit that, in exceptional cases, the Spirit may now operate directly, indepen-
dent of the word, in disposing a soul to engage in the work of
the ministry, without surrendering the point at issue, and open-
ing the door of admission to the mystics and enthusiasts.

DEMITTING THE MINISTRY.

In the Romish hierarchy, the priests constitute a permanent clerical *order*, none of whom is allowed to lay down his
priesthood. The Church of England imbibed, with episcopacy,
the Romish idea, that a clergyman could not be relieved from

the sacred functions assumed at his ordination, and the British
Parliament passed a law declaring that "a priest or deacon could
not, and ought not to divest himself of his clerical character."
In 1773, Rev. Horne Took divested himself of his clerical robe,
studied law, but was refused admission to the bar. He was subsequently elected to Parliament, and although his claim to a
seat was at first resisted on the ground that he was still a clergyman, he was afterwards admitted. This case, however, became the occasion of the passage of an act declaring the ineli-
gibility of persons in his situation. The Lutheran Church, re-
garding the ministry not as a clerical order, but as an office of
special service in the Christian Church, maintains that should
an individual, under a conviction of duty, be inducted into the
ministry, and be afterwards providentially prevented from discharging its duties, he has the right to lay down the office of
the ministry, and the body which invested him with it has the
authority to relieve him of its obligations, to divest him of its
title, and restore him to the position of a layman in the congregation.

This view of the subject is based upon the constitution of the
Christian Church, whose members are called to perform various
kinds of service in different offices. If now a person be disabled from performing the duties of one office, and be able to
perform those of another, he has not only the right, but it becomes his duty, to lay down the one and assume those of the
other office. Philip devoted himself at first to the office of a deacon, but afterward relinquished it and became an evangelist. If
this had been reversed, he would have had the right, for adequate reasons, to relinquish the office of an evangelist and re-
assume that of a deacon, or to become again a layman.

This view of the office of the ministry is a legitimate development of the doctrine of the priesthood of all believers.
Christians constitute a universal priesthood, each one of whom
is endowed with talents fitting him for the performance of some
particular service, and some of whom are qualified and called to
devote themselves to the special work of the ministry. Should
any one of the latter discover, after a full trial, that he has missed
his calling, or be so disabled that he cannot continue to preach

and administer the sacraments, and that he is able and compelled to engage in some secular pursuit to make a living, he has the right to ask, and it becomes the duty of the ecclesiastical body to which he belongs, to release him from his ordination vows, which he cannot meet, and to allow him to take his place again among the common priesthood, and to perform such service as his gifts, means and circumstances will permit. The Lutheran view of the subject has made such progress in England that Parliament passed a law entitled "The Clerical Disability Act," in 1870, according to whose provisions any minister of the Church of England may resign his preferment, and resume again the position of a layman.

The following incident, narrated by Dr. Thomas Guthrie in his *Sunday Magazine*, must have occurred at the time when this act was under consideration, and comes in point in this discussion :

"In making statements against the retention in the ministry of those who are unfitted for it, at a dinner table where a bishop was present, I was met by one appealing to him how that could be, seeing that every candidate for holy orders, in seeking them, declared himself to be moved by the Holy Ghost? An objection to the bill brought into the House of Lords for allowing clergymen of the English Church to demit their office and loose themselves of their ordination vows, which I met with was this, namely, that such candidates must have been mistaken, since God never calls a man by his Spirit to any office for which he is not fit."

In the United States a similar change of opinion and practice has been inaugurated. About twenty years ago, a Methodist bishop in the South asked to lay down his bishopric, and after a full discussion of the subject, his request was granted by the House of Bishops. Consistency with the views of the Lutheran Church on the call to the ministry, demands that she should, under similar circumstances, take the same course. Accordingly, the Ministerium of Pennsylvania, at its annual session in 1870, relieved one of its members of the clerical office, and the East Pennsylvania Synod did the same at its meeting in the fall of the same year. And several similar cases have occurred since.

The right to abdicate the ministerial office ought not, however, to be exercised at random or from caprice, nor granted without good and sufficient reasons. Men called to devote themselves to pursuits cognate to those of the ministry, such as teachers, professors and editors, may consistently continue in the ministerial profession. But when a man, in his youth or the prime of life is disabled from discharging the duties of the ministry, and is necessitated and able to prosecute some secular calling for life, it becomes his duty to ask, and that of the synod to grant him, the privilege of demitting his office. But should a minister not thus disabled, from choice and worldly motives, devote himself to business for life, he would prostitute the holy office, imitate the example of Demas, if not of Judas, and, should he not voluntarily demit the ministry, ought to be divested of its name and functions.

The opposite view is as unreasonable as it is unscriptural. It compels a man to bear a name which becomes a misnomer, and to retain an office, with its solemn responsibilities, whose duties he knows he can never again perform. It exposes him, in some degree at least, among those ignorant of his disability, to the odium that attaches to a clergyman who abandons the ministry for the sake of filthy lucre, and even prevents his highest usefulness as a layman. Hence the ministerial office becomes to him a sinecure, its name an unmeaning sound, its solemn vows a disturber of his conscience, and its ecclesiastical relations and duties a serious inconvenience, if not an oppressive burden.

STATISTICS SHOWING THE PRACTICAL WORKING OF BOTH SYSTEMS.

As a tree is known by its fruits, the respective character of the two theories we are contrasting will become manifest by a comparison of their results. The subjoined statistics setting forth the proportion of the number of ministers to the number of the communicants in the Presbyterian, Congregational and Unitarian denominations, as well as those of the Lutheran Church, reveal the legitimate results of both systems, and constitute a practical balance in which they may be duly weighed.

Dr. Herrick Johnson, in his sermon as Moderator of the last General Assembly of the Presbyterian Church, said: "We are threatened with a famine of the ministry. We have 5,744 churches, and, take every pastor, stated supply, home and foreign missionary now in the field, and there are yet 2,000 churches uncared for. Add all the retired ministers, presidents, professors, teachers, editors, etc., and there are still 601 churches without a shepherd. In the last ten years one-third of the increase in our ministry has been due to accessions from other denominations. We are making less ministers than we made ten years ago. The Church is losing her grip on the Christian colleges as nurseries of ministerial candidates.

"What is the cause of the steadily lessening number of ministerial candidates? It is not the trials of the ministry, nor its inadequate support; not the inducement of brilliant prospects in other callings, nor the intellectual demands made upon the ministry; not the lack of adequate provision on the part of our Church for collegiate education, nor chiefly the lack of general Christian conversation. It is still the same peril I have talked of—the peril of truth's perversion, of losing the spirit in the form."

The *Interior* published Dr. Johnson's sermon, accompanied with the following significant comments and portentous facts and figures:

"We are losing ground. For ten years we have almost every year declined from the record of the preceding year in number of candidates for the ministry.

"Comparing the colleges for the past ten years presents a most discouraging exhibit. The number of graduates is increasing, but steadily the number of those who look toward the ministry is decreasing.

"But the most astounding facts come into view in comparing the number of candidates for the ministry from the different sections of the church. Thus in the southern section, where are the colored churches under the care of the Freedmen's Board, and in the foreign field together, there is one candidate to every two hundred and fifteen communicants; in the western section of the country there is one to every nine hundred and sixty-six; and in the eastern section one to every twelve hundred and fourteen. That is to say, the colored churches and the foreign mission churches furnish nearly twenty per cent. of the ministers; while in the old Presbyterian centers, with more than a hundred years of Presbyterian history, and a handy supply of the very best schools and colleges, the number of candidates is alarmingly small, and steadily decreasing. Brooklyn Presbytery, with almost twelve thousand communicants, has only two candidates. Erie, with nearly eight thousand, has not one candidate on the way to the ministry; and the whole Synod of Michigan, outside of Detroit, with more than ten thousand communicants, has only one candidate."

A writer in the *Atlantic Monthly*, on "The Decline of Congregationalism," shows that while the population of the United States has increased twelve millions or thirty-three and a third per cent., the Congregational Church has not kept pace with this ratio, having increased only twenty-three per cent., or two and three-tenths per cent. per annum, while some of the other Protestant churches have increased more than twice as much proportionally as the population of this country, and we might add, that in this respect the Lutheran Church excels them all, having increased during the last decade nearly one hundred per cent. And that the proportionate decline in the membership of the Congregational Church indicates a corresponding decline in her candidates for the ministry, is evident from the gradual decrease of their number in the graduating classes of Yale, and the conclusion is that this decline is general as given in the following extract from the *New York Observer* :

"Of eighty-five professors of religion in the last graduating class at Yale—there were in all 149—only five express an intention to study for the ministry. This is a very small number. Does it not indicate on the part of young educated men, a decline of interest in the ministerial profession? It is far below the average of former years, especially the early years of American colleges. We fear that the decline is general, and it is time to ask the reason for it."

Nor is this decrease in the ministry confined to the orthodox churches, but exists in a still greater degree among the Unitarians, as indicated by the following statements made by a candidate for the ministry in Harvard:

"The decrease in the number of students who study for the ministry is very marked. It seems strange that out of so many young men, representing all classes of society, and every shade of belief or unbelief, so few choose the work of advancing the kingdom of God. Nothing can show the steady decrease so forcibly as a few figures. Between 1642 and 1650, 53 per cent. of the graduates entered the ministry. Between 1861 and 1870, 7 per cent. Down to 1701 the per cent. of graduates entering the ministry was 52. In the eighteenth century it was 29 per cent. In the first seven decades of the nineteenth century it was 11 per cent. During the last ten years only 4 per cent. have chosen the profession which we have in view. In my class there were seven out of 177 graduates. Here is a falling off in a ratio of 13 to 1 in two hundred years."

While America is threatened with a famine in the ministry, Germany has been favored with a special ingathering. With the recent revival of orthodoxy and evangelical piety, the number of candidates has greatly increased. In verification of this gratifying fact, we quote the following testimony, taken from the *Sunday-School Times* of July 7th :

"Now when the cry is going up from the theological seminaries of the various denominations in America, that the supply of ministers is falling short of the enlarged demand here, and that even a smaller proportion of college graduates than formerly is entering the ministerial profession, it is encouraging to look away to what has happened in Germany, and what is now happening there. Germany has already passed through that state of spiritual dearth which many are now fearing for this country. There was a time when the cause of Christianity seemed to the fearful to be almost lost in Germany. But within the past few years a change for the better has showed itself. Sunday-schools are spreading ; the cities are being stirred by evangelistic movements; and the study of theology is once more attracting the more scholarly youth of Germany. Since 1876, the number of theological students in the nine Prussian universities has more than doubled. Great as this increase is, it seems all the greater when compared with the increase in other than the theological faculties. The number of students of philosophy, and of law, in the Prussian universities, increased last year less than two per cent. each; and of medicine, less than fifteen per cent.; while the students of Roman Catholic theology increased in number nearly ten per cent. and those of Protestant theology more than twenty-one per cent. These figures would certainly seem to show a return towards Christianity on the part of German students; and they certainly mark a new stirring of the spiritual life among the people. If it be true, as has been claimed, that we have latterly taken our fashions in skepticism and in theology from Germany, and that the present relative falling off in the number of theological students is due to the influence of that form of skepticism which is now going to pieces in the country that gave it birth, what may we not look for in the near future, now that Germany is setting us a better fashion in the way in which the higher class of young men are there pressing forward into the ministry of the Christian Church."

The following are the statistics of the Lutheran Church in this country showing the number of candidates for the ministry in her principal Theological Seminaries and Colleges.

GENERAL SYNOD NORTH.

In the eight district synods represented in the Theological Seminary at Gettysburg there are 86,039 members. The number of students in the seminary, from these synods, is 26, and from other sections of the Church 11, an aggregate of 37, of whom 17 are beneficiaries. During the last ten years, the average number of theological students entering and leaving the seminary is about 11, an aggregate of 110.

In the regular classes of Pennsylvania College at Gettysburg, there are 107 students, of whom 47 are candidates for the ministry, which with 2 in the preparatory department, makes an aggregate of 49.

In the Theological Department of the Missionary Institute, at Selinsgrove, Pa., there are 13 students, of whom 6 receive aid from the Church; and in the Classical Department there are 15 with the ministry in view. The number of ministers sent forth from the institution during the last ten years is 47, of whom 30 were beneficiaries.

The number of communicants in the three synods in the States of New York and New Jersey is 15,139. At Hartwick Seminary, there are 5 students in the theological and 7 in the preparatory department, who intend studying for the ministry. Since 1876, 6 have entered the ministry, and 2 more will complete their course this year.

The number of members in the five synods supporting Wittenberg College is 19,606. The number of students in the theological department of Wittenberg College is 7, and the number sent forth during the last ten years is 60. In the collegiate department there are about 30 students who have resolved to prepare themselves for the ministry, a total of 37.

There are six Lutheran synods in connection with Carthage College, Illinois, containing 9,261 members. During the last ten years, 5 young men from these synods have entered the Lutheran ministry, and 2 that of other denominations, and there were 5 students in Carthage College in 1882–3 who were candidates for the ministry, out of 26 in the classical department, 3 of whom were beneficiaries.

GENERAL SYNOD SOUTH.

The General Synod South numbers about 18,000 members. All its district synods are formally pledged to the support of the Theological Seminary at Salem, Va. There are 10 students in the seminary, of whom 8 are beneficiaries. The number of theological students that have entered the seminary, since its removal to Salem, ten years ago, is 54. Of the 100 students in the regular classes of Roanoke College, 13 have the ministry in view. In Newberry College, Newberry, S. C., there are 8 candidates for the ministry out of 25 students in the college classes.

GENERAL COUNCIL.

The number of communicants in the General Council is 196,-948. There are at present 52 students in the Theological Seminary in Philadelphia. During the last ten years there were graduated from this institution 148, and hospitants (students taking an elective course, but not matriculated), 18. During the last five years the Pennsylvania Synod supported 54 students in the Seminary in Philadelphia and 72 in Muhlenberg College, a total of 126—or an average of about 25 a year.

In the regular classes of Muhlenberg College there are 74 students, 39 of whom propose to devote themselves to the ministry. There are also 4 in the preparatory, making 43 in all.

Thiel College Greenville, Pa., has, since its organization thirteen years ago, furnished 25 ministers, and has 12 theological students in the Philadelphia Seminary. There are at present 30 candidates for the ministry in the institution. In the college classes there are 43 young men, 23 of whom are candidates for the ministry, 14 being self-supporting and 9 beneficiaries. There are 12 candidates in the preparatory department, 9 of whom are self-supporting and 3 beneficiaries.

The Swedish Augustana Synod numbers 50,991 communicants. There are in the theological department of Augustana College, at Rock Island, Ill., 35 students, and in the collegiate department there are 80 students, 50 of whom are designed for the ministry. These all are supported by supplies and contributions from the congregations. During the last ten years 103 candidates have been educated and ordained by the synod.

INDEPENDENT SYNODS.

The Joint Synod of Ohio has 50,600 members. There are 39 students in its Theological Seminary, at Columbus, O., about two-thirds of whom receive support from the churches, and 90 ministers have been sent forth from it during the last ten years. In Capital University there are 41 students in the college classes, four-fifths of whom have the ministry in view.

The German Synod of Iowa has 25,000 members. There are in the theological department of Mendota College 59 students, all of whom, with rare exceptions, receive aid from the congregations, and 17 in the gymnasium, nearly all of whom are preparing for the study of theology. As the number of candidates for the ministry furnished by the congregations of the synod, is not adequate to provide them with pastors, from six to ten young men, in various stages of preparation for the ministry, in the gymnasia and theological institutions in Germany, are sent to Mendota, where they complete their studies and enter the mission field of the synod, mostly in the northwest. Nor is this all. The Lutherans in Germany, with whom the Iowa Synod keeps up an ecclesiastical correspondence, not only furnish young men, but also provide the means to sustain them, and one-third of the students in the seminary are supported from the beneficiary treasury of Mecklenburg and the contributions of a few other congregations.

THE JOINT SYNOD OF MISSOURI.

The Missouri Synod has 185,000 members. In its principal Theological Seminary, at St. Louis, Mo., there are 105 students, two-thirds of whom are sustained by their parents or friends, one-sixth by the congregations from which they come, and one-sixth from a common beneficiary treasury. At their Pro-Theological Seminary, at Springfield, Ill., there are 184 students. In the Gymnasium (College), at Fort Wayne, Ind., there are about 200 students. In the five Pro-Gymnasia, or College Institutes, there are 114 students, preparing for admission into the Gymnasium, at Fort Wayne. All the students last mentioned, whether pursuing the regular course in college or preparing for it in the collegiate institutes, are, with here and there an exception, preparing for the ministry. In their Teachers' Seminaries, or Normal Schools, there are 156 students, preparing themselves as teachers in the parochial schools of the congregations. These students also study theology to some extent, and are thoroughly drilled in Dietrich's Catechism, the confessions of our church, etc., and are pledged to these confessions in the call extended to them, and are thus fitted to give proper instruction in the catechism, Bible history, and kindred subjects. The summary of these statistics is as follows: Theological students, 289; candidates for the ministry in course of preparation, 314; total, 603; students in Teachers' Seminaries, 156; grand total, 759.

The statistics above given, furnish the data for the following comparative statements, showing that, other things being equal, just in proportion as the true, or Lutheran theory of a call to the ministry, has been adopted, and the Lutheran methods to develop it have been carried out in the family, the parochial school, the catechetical class, and the congregation, in that proportion, has the number of the candidates for the ministry been increased, and just in proportion as the prevalent theory has been adopted, and the Lutheran view and methods abandoned, in that proportion has the number of candidates for the ministry decreased.

The General Synod North has 130,000 communicants, and 168 candidates for the ministry in its institutions, being 1 for every 774 communicants.

The General Council, excluding the Augustana Synod, has 145,957 communicants and 130 candidates, being 1 for every 1,123 communicants.

The Swedish Augustana Synod of the General Council has 50,991 communicants and 85 candidates, being 1 for every 600 communicants.

The General Synod South has 18,000 communicants and 31 candidates, being 1 in every 581.

The Joint Synod of Ohio has 50,600 communicants and 71 candidates, being 1 for every 713.

The German Synod of Iowa has 25,000 communicants and 76 candidates, being 1 for every 330.

The Missouri Synod has 185,000 communicants and 603 candidates, being 1 for every 307 communicants.

The aggregate number of communicants in the synods named above is 605,548, and the number of candidates for the ministry 1,164, or about 1 for every 520 communicants, revealing the fact that the three European Synods—the Swedish Augustana, the German Synod of Iowa, and the Missouri Synod—with 260,991 communicants, have 764 candidates, being 1 for every 342 communicants; and that the American Synods—the General Synods North and South, the General Council and the Joint Synod of Ohio—with 344,557 members, have 400 candidates, or one for every 861 communicants; and that the Missouri Synod, with 185,000 communicants, has more candidates for the ministry than the General Synod North and South, the General Council, the Joint Synod of Ohio, and the German Synod of Iowa combined, with 420,548 communicants.

The following comparative statements of the number of ministers sent out by the Lutheran ecclesiastical bodies mentioned above, during the last ten years, exhibits about the same relative proportion.

The General Synod North has sent forth from its institutions, during the last ten years, 228 ministers, being one annually for every 5700 communicants.

The General Council, not including the Swedish Augustana Synod, has sent out during the same time 251, being one annually for every 7850.

The Swedish Augustana Synod has sent out 103, being one annually for every 4950.

The General Synod South has sent out 54, being one annually for every 3330.

The Joint Synod of Ohio has sent out 90, being one annually for every 7850.

The German Synod of Iowa has sent out 70, being one annually for every 3570.

The Missouri Synod has sent out about 500, being one annually for every 3700.

In corroboration of the statements just made, we present the following survey of the views and practices, prevalent in the different Lutheran ecclesiastical bodies in the United States.

The General Synod, the oldest of the Lutheran general bodies in America, has generally adopted the prevalent theory, and its practice has been governed by it. Its results in the States of New York and New Jersey, Prof. James Pitcher, Principal of the Classical Department of Hartwick Seminary, describes as follows:

"In 1876-7, there was but one young man from the synods in the states of New York and New Jersey studying for the ministry, and he was in Pennsylvania College, at Gettysburg, and has since taken a theological course and is now in the ministry. In 1878-9 there were 4 students having the ministry in view at Hartwick Seminary; in 1879-80, there were 11; in 1880-81, there were 15; in 1881-2, there were but 12; and this number has been maintained in the last two years. There are at present 3 candidates for the ministry from the State of New York, studying in other literary and theological institutions."

In Pennsylvania and Maryland, Ohio and the adjacent States, under the direct influence of Pennsylvania College and the Theological Seminary, the Missionary Institute and Wittenberg College, the best showing in that body is presented; while in the far West, on the territory of Carthage College, a more discouraging exhibit is made.

In the English and Pennsylvania German churches of the General Council the prevalent theory has also held the sway, but the Lutheran theory is dominant in its German and Scandinavian churches; and while their influence, in this respect, is making itself felt in the English churches, its ministerial statistics indicate a marked and hopeful advance. And in this respect, Thiel College, although but thirteen years old, presents a remarkable ministerial record, which stands in striking contrast with that of Carthage College, only a few years younger.

Scandinavian and German Lutheran bodies in this country have generally not only adopted the Lutheran theory, but also developed it by Lutheran methods. The Swedish Augustana Synod is a fair representative of the views and practices that prevail among the Swedes and Norwegians. Dr. Hasselquist, President of Augustana College and Seminary, Rock Island, Ills., furnished us the data for the following statements.

Among the pious Scandinavian Lutheran families, many parents are desirous that at least one of their sons shall serve the Lord in his vineyard, and when they see such talents in them as would fit them for the ministry, they encourage them to study, in order that they may discover the will of God concerning them. Teachers of the parochial schools pursue a similar course with talented boys, and pastors do the same with their catechumens; and on this wise natural and spiritual traits, constituting the marks of a call to the ministry, are discerned in the boys and nurtured in the young men, culminating in a conviction that they are called to the ministry, and are sent forth approved by parents, teachers and pastors.

Dr. Sigmund Fritschel, President of Mendota College and Seminary, Illinois, gave us an interesting account of the operations of the German Lutheran Synod of Iowa, from which we present the following digest:

It is imposed upon pastors by the synod, as a duty, to look out for talented and pious young men, giving promise of adaptation for the ministry, to confer with their parents on the subject, and to see to it, that they be sent to the College at Mendota. The younger boys of this class are first sent to the Teachers' Seminary, at Beverly, Ia., where they are taught the rudiments of an education, and such as develop the necessary traits of mind and heart, and are then sent to the college and seminary, at Mendota. Pious German Lutheran parents appreciate the ministry, and are gratified when one or more of their sons are deemed worthy to enter it, and such as are able, cheerfully support them during their preparatory studies. The parochial school, with its educated Christian teacher and positive religious instruction in the catechism and the Scriptures, is also brought into requisition, in discovering the elect sons of the congregation and pointing them out to the pastors, who, through a thorough course of catechetical instruction, are able to test both their talents and their piety, and to assist them in coming to a just conclusion concerning their call to the ministry as a profession for life.

The Missouri Synod is the largest and wealthiest among our German ecclesiastical bodies. It has adopted and carried out in the most rigid manner and to the greatest extent the Lutheran theory of the ministry, and both the number and the character of the ministers they are calling out and educating, challenge special attention.

The teachers of the parochial schools have the best opportunity of finding out the most promising boys, and of calling their attention to the work of the ministry. They also confer with their parents on the subject, and encourage them to educate them for the holy office. The general result of this whole system of religious training in the family, the catechetical class and the parochial school, in its bearing on the call to the ministry, is thus described by Rev. H. Walker, pastor of St. John's German Lutheran church, York, Pa., to whose kind offices we are indebted for the statistics heretofore given and the facts stated above. "Although now and then," says he, "a boy does not turn out as well as was expected, and must, therefore, be dismissed from the institution, yet, as a rule, they come up fully to our expectations and hopes, and, by the grace of God, become well educated, faithful ministers and teachers in church and school."

The subjoined extract from a letter written by Dr. S. A. Repass, Professor in the Southern Theological Seminary, after a conversation had with him in Virginia last summer reveals the true state of things in the Southern churches, and abounds with such judicious reflections that we present them as the results of his experience and observation for many years:

The points in the conversation which you desired noted were these: *The small number of young men preparing for the ministry, and the cause of this.* As to the first, I had stated that from one of the largest synods in our Southern Church only one student was in the Seminary at Salem during the past year, and one at Gettysburg; that I could not at that time recall any in our college who were preparing for the holy office; that from another synod there would be no representation the coming session, and perhaps none the session of '84-'85. In another of our synods only one student has been in the seminary here—and none elsewhere—since it was transferred, a period of ten years, although from this same synod come frequent appeals for men. The same might be said, with very few exceptions, of our Church in general in the South. Appalling as these statements are, they apply, according to your own confession, to the Lutheran Church in other portions of the country. In fact, as large a proportion, perhaps somewhat larger, extending the comparison over several years, enter the ministry from our Southern Church as from any of the *English* portion of the Church North. But we can find no comfort in such statistics. Rather does the comparison increase our shame, in view of the fact of the destitution facing us everywhere.

We spoke also of the cause of this state of things. There must be something radically wrong in the system, or the one now in operation is miserably worked. That a congregation fifty or seventy-five years old should in all that time furnish no candidates—and we know of some such—cannot be according to the will of God, except, indeed, we interpret that will as a judgment. The opinion was confidently expressed that there is and has been most culuable neglect in our pastors in presenting the claims of the ministry upon the Church. The opinion practically obtains that the Church has little to do in the matter apart from authorizing those who apply, or in educating such as make up their minds to the belief that they are called. The view was expressed that the current notion on this subject did not operate healthfully; that it kept out of the ministry some of our best young men; that almost all who enter are dependent upon the Church for help. Whilst not saying aught against beneficiary education, there is certainly something abnormal in the facts as they present themselves, viz., that so very, very few of our ministers come out of our wealthier families. It is wresting the word of God to quote here this, "not many mighty, etc., are called," for there is no Scripture to warrant the conclusion that God has excluded from the privilege and honor of preaching the Gospel those who are able to educate themselves.

CONCLUDING REMARKS.

The ministerial statistics of the Presbyterian Church, given above, exhibit in an unmistakable manner, that the practical tendency of the prevalent theory is, to decrease the number of the candidates for the ministry, until the supply gives out and famine prevails. That in such a Church, with its intelligence, wealth, institutions, and educative funds, the number of candidates for the ministry could run down to two, in the Presbytery of Brooklyn with twelve thousand communicants, to one in the Synod of Michigan with ten thousand, and to zero in the Presbytery of Erie with eight thousand, proves beyond question, that a theory under whose practical operation such results are possible, cannot be the true one, and must prove disastrous to the Church. And this exhibit becomes the more remarkable, when it is considered, that this threatened famine in the ministry, has occurred in the largest, best equipped and most influential Calvinistic denomination in this country. And as, according to the Calvinistic doctrine of election and grace, God not only determines the individual number of the elect, but also the means by which they are effectually called and persevere unto salvation, and as the calling of an adequate number of ministers to preach the Gospel, through which every one of the elect must be brought to a saving knowledge of the truth, is indispensable, it would seem that God has either overlooked the pastoral wants of his elect people, by calling so few ministers among them through the direct influence of the Spirit, or else it must be concluded, either that those called did not understand the import of the impulse of the Spirit, or that, understanding it, they all with one consent made excuses, and refused to obey it.

The particularity of the prevalent theory accords, indeed, with the Calvinistic doctrine of a limited atonement and election, according to which the number of the redeemed and elect is comparatively so small, that a correspondingly small number of ministers is needed to preach to them the Gospel, and hence the Spirit, who limits his effectual call to the few elect, confines his direct call to the ministry to the very small number predestinated as the elect ministers of Christ. But it cannot be made to harmonize with the universality of the Lutheran doctrine of the atonement, of the call of the Gospel, of the Spirit, and of the priesthood of all believers, according to which, the Church is bound to call forth and send out an adequate number of ministers to preach the Gospel to every creature, in order that, according to the universal purpose of God's free grace, none should perish, but that all should be brought to repentance and salvation.

The gradual diminution of the number of the ministry in the Presbyterian and other Puritanic denominations, in America, while it may well startle them, is not, when duly considered, at all strange. It is the legitimate outgrowth of the prevalent theory of a call to the ministry. In the natural world no end can be rationally expected and attained, unless the adopted means for its accomplishment are employed in a timely and propitious manner. And the same law has been established in the supernatural world. Conviction of sin, as an end, cannot be expected on the part of the Spirit, the reprover of sin, unless a knowledge of the truth concerning the law, as the means of the Spirit, be made known by the Church. Faith in Christ, as an end, cannot be reasonably expected, unless the truths concerning the person and work of Christ, as the revealed instrumentality of the Spirit, be proclaimed by the Church. Should the Church fall into the error, that the Spirit would reprove the world of sin, and work faith in Christ directly, without the written word, which he moved the holy men of God to reveal for this very purpose, and consequently neglect to promulgate it, their hopes would be disappointed, and sinners remain in their ignorance and unbelief. And this is just the folly and inconsistency into which these churches have fallen, in adopting and relying upon the prevalent theory for an adequate supply of able and successful ministers, through the direct call of the Spirit, instead of his indirect call, through the dissemination and practical development by the Church of the truths revealed in the Scriptures, and inspired by the Spirit, concerning the qualifications which constitute the infallible mark of his call to the ministry.

The family is the divinely appointed nursery of the ministry. Those called to it are entrusted to parents for their education, religious training, and judicious direction in matters pertaining to their vocation and course of life. But how lamentably is all this overlooked in most of our families! Many parents neglect the education of their children, or trust their religious instruction to others, fail to impress upon their minds the true object of life, refuse to dedicate their gifted sons to the ministry, and instead of urging upon them its claims, rather prejudice them against it. And should any of their sons, under other influences, resolve to study for the ministry, in spite of such inexcusable indifference, fathers not unfrequently refuse to support them and even mothers turn a deaf ear to their entreaties for help. And while they thus withhold their able bodied, strong minded sons from the service of the Lord who made and bought them with his blood, should one of them be possessed of a feeble constitution and a weak mind, they prevail upon him to choose the ministry, as an easy way of making a living.

In the patriarchal age, the first born son, in every family, was set apart as the priest of the household, and in apostolic times, it was believed that sons of some families were called to the

ministry in every Christian congregation, but under the prevailing theory of a call to the ministry, it occurs that, not only
in the great majority of families, but in scores of congregations,
yea, in whole synods, not a single candidate for the ministry is
brought out.

. The primitive churches embraced the true theory of a call to
the ministry. Accordingly they believed, that an adequate
number of men was called not only to supply each congregation with one or more pastors, but also to provide missionaries
to go forth, organize and supply other congregations. Under
this procedure, inaugurated•by Christ and his apostles, Christianity was rapidly made known through Palestine, Asia Minor,
Greece and Rome, and but for a departure from it, would long
ago have encompassed the habitable globe. Under the opposite theory, it is believed, that in scores of congregations containing many hundreds of talented and pious young men, only
here and there one, is called to the ministry, and it is regarded
neither as a reproach nor a calamity, that large and wealthy
congregations should send forth no candidates for the ministry,
during ten, twenty, fifty, years, yea, during their entire history.

Were but the lowest number, namely two, regarded as called
by the apostles who ordained "elders," in each of the primitive
churches, it would give the General Synod with its thirteen
hundred and fifty congregations twenty-seven hundred candidates for the ministry; and the Lutheran Church in this country with its six thousand, three hundred churches, twelve thousand six hundred young men called to the ministry. It would
revolutionize its aggressive character, enable it to supply all its
destitution at home and take its appropriate position in the
prosecution of the work of converting the world.

Parents on presenting their children to God obligate themselves to bring them up in the *faith* in which they were baptized, in other words, they solemnly covenanted with God to
give them a Christian education. The necessity and importance
of establishing parochial schools by Christian congregations,
and the duty of parents to see to it that their children receive a
thorough religious training in them, are both involved in In-
fant Baptism. In Europe full provision is made in this respect,

and the parochial school was brought by our fathers to America, and their establishment was enjoined by constitutional provision upon every Lutheran congregation. A school-house became a necessary appendage to every church. The Scandinavian and the Germans, as we have seen, encourage their congregations to establish and support parochial schools. The English Lutheran churches, and a goodly number of the Pennsylvania German Lutheran congregations, have given up the parochial, and availed themselves of the common schools, as their substitute. But the best of these schools, in which the Bible is still read, the Lord's Prayer repeated, and Christian hymns sung, are so deficient in positive religious instructions, that they cannot possibly give a child even a general religious training, and those schools from which the Bible has been excluded cannot be styled Christian in any proper sense. The inconsistency of the Church, in turning her baptized children over to the State, which can give little more than a secular education, instead of providing religious schools herself, and giving them a positively Christian education, must be apparent to all. And the superficial notion, that our Sunday-schools constitute an adequate substitute for the common school, and that scarce an hour's religious instruction on Sunday can make up for its neglect during all its school hours in the week, is proven to be deceptive by the opinions and conduct of the children educated in these schools. And the practical effect of the parochial and the common school systems on the number and character of our ministry, the reader will see by a comparison of the statistics furnished by each as given heretofore.

The pulpit should not only be the guardian, but the efficient propagator of the ministry. Its opportunities and advantages for presenting, at proper times and in all manner of forms, the truths concerning the call, character, service and blessed results of the work of the ministry, and of urging its claims upon young men, and its due appreciation upon all church members are so numerous and great, that the expectation would naturally be cherished, that they would do full justice to their own office. But under the demoralizing influence of the prevalent theory of. •

a call to the ministry, its incumbents fold their hands and wait for the Spirit to give the call, instead of looking out for the marks of the call, in the talents and graces conferred, and of making intelligent efforts to convince the young men possessing them that they are called, and ought to devote themselves to the ministry. And we question whether one of our ministers in fifty has ever preached on the call to the ministry, and urged its claims from the Lutheran standpoint.

The repeated and various forms in which the religious press is adapted to present the Church and her service, the ministry and its claims, Christian nurture in the family, religious training in the school, the value of a sanctified literature, and the achievements made in the mission field of the world, render it the most powerful agency, and efficient assistant to parents, teachers, church officers and pastors, in disseminating religious intelligence, calculated to awaken attention to the office of the ministry, to exhibit its true characteristics, to incite efforts on its behalf, and to induce many young men to choose it as their profession for life. But so illiterate and penurious are many of our church members, that they can neither appreciate the character, nor estimate the value of a first-class church paper to themselves and their households, and as a consequence not more than one family out of four or five, and not more than one member in fifteen or twenty, can be induced to take the *Observer*. In these families the door is barred to all religious intelligence, and as the parents know little or nothing about the Church and her work, they take little or no interest in it, and as the sons read nothing about the ministry, and hear nothing but complaining and disparaging criticisms of their pastor, they lose all respect for the office and never entertain even a thought, that the talents and graces conferred upon them, would enable them to render God service in the ministry and that it is their duty to prepare for and prosecute it as their life work.

That God has not discriminated in favor of the sons of the wealthy, to the disparagement of those of the poor, in conferring constitutional and gracious endowments, and that he has, .consequently, called many poor as well as rich young men into the ministry, needs no proof. That all such require both literary and theological culture for the successful prosecution of its work is equally apparent. The necessity of providing the means for the education of indigent, talented, and pious young men, becomes consequently, manifest, and the duty of contributing to this cause to such a degree that no worthy candidate possessing the evident marks of God's call imprinted upon his intellectual, physical and moral constitution need be rejected.

Notwithstanding this, the contributions of the churches have been for many years inadequate to educate the acceptable candidates presenting themselves, under the operation of the prevalent theory of a call to the ministry, to say nothing of the scores and hundreds of young men, endowed with the necessary qualifications, who might have been brought out by proper efforts, and educated for the ministry, according to the true theory, if the means had been provided. But so large has been the number of beneficiaries, who proved failures, on account of their improprieties in conduct as students, deficiency of intellect, blemishes of character, slowness of speech, and lack of common sense, as to bring the whole system into disrepute, in spite of the large numbers, educated by the Church, who have proven themselves worthy and successful ministers of Christ. In the discussion of the subject, thus called forth, some have suggested that the Church should provide for the education of large numbers of her young men, and then select those possessed of the requisite abilities, and endeavor to convince them of their call to the ministry. Others have maintained, that the temptations held out to young men to choose the ministry as a means of obtaining an education and bettering their chances for life, are so strong and the number of those who failed to refund the money advanced them for their education, after they had become able to do it, so great, that this plan had better be abandoned as found wanting.

Two years ago, the Pennsylvania Synod abandoned the system of beneficiary education, as such, and now only advances money to such as need and apply for assistance, taking their notes, without interest, and relying upon their honor to refund the sums loaned, after they enter the ministry. The result, thus far, has been, that the number of applicants has been

greatly reduced, an illustration of which is found in the five candidates of the Freshman class of Muhlenberg College, not one
of whom has applied for aid and all of whom support themselves. But so long as the Church fails to select her candidates,
according to the marks of a call pointed out by the Scriptures,
and waits until those claiming to have received a direct call
from the Spirit, offer themselves, these failures will be repeated,
in spite of any other expedients that may be adopted, and the
discrepancy between the number of the laborers and the extent
of the harvest continue.

Self-protection has compelled the churches, in a measure, at
least, to discredit the reliability of the direct call, and by sub-
jecting all applicants for aid, to a preparatory course of training at their own expense, adequate to fit them for College, and
without which, as a practical test, they cannot be received on
the funds of the synod, the result of which has been, that the
number of applicants has been considerably reduced. For example, in the East Pennsylvania Synod, with 13,616 communicants, there was but one candidate for the ministry, who applied
for assistance. There was, consequently a balance of more than
$2,200 in the beneficiary treasury, awaiting applicants, and no
assessment was, accordingly made for beneficiary education in
1883–4. And when it is recollected that this synod includes
the cities of Philadelphia, Lancaster, Harrisburg, Pottsville,
Reading, Allentown, and Easton, the outlook for the supply
of ministers is not reassuring. And although the above require-
ment was a step in the right direction, the system cannot be relieved of all defects, until the true theory of a call to the ministry be restored, and the Church select her candidates, instead
of accepting those who offer themselves, footing the bills, and
taking all the risk.

The beneficiary system, in its practical results, has not only
made itself liable to objections such as have just been referred
to, but it has become the occasion of a wide spread impression
that the Church must get her candidates for the ministry from
the families of the poor and educate them at her expense, while
the majority of families of the wealthy refuse, on this account,
to induce their talented and pious sons to devote themselves

to the ministry, and educate them rather for any other profession. In corroboration of these statements, we present the following statistics, showing what proportion of the students in our theological, and of the candidates in our literary institutions, come from our wealthy families and support themselves, and what proportion are drawn from the families of the poor, and are supported by the Church.

Ten years ago, the startling fact was stated to us by Dr. J. A. Brown, that there was not a single theological student in the seminary at Gettysburg, who was supported by his parents or friends, and that all were beneficiaries. It is matter of gratification that a marked improvement has taken place in this respect since that time. Of the 37 theological students now at Gettysburg, 20 are supported by their parents, and 17 are beneficiaries. Of 49 candidates for the ministry in Pennsylvania College, 25 are beneficiaries. Of 13 theological students at the Missionary Institute, 7 are self-supported, and 6 receive aid from the churches. Of 15 candidates in the classical department 10 support themselves and 5 are beneficiaries. Of 7 students in the theological department of Wittenberg College, 3 support themselves and 4 are beneficiaries, and of 30 candidates in the college 15 are self-supported, and 15 are beneficiaries. In Carthage College of the 5 candidates for the ministry, 2 are self-supported and 3 are beneficiaries. In the German Theological Seminary at Chicago, 7 students are reported, all of whom receive assistance from the Church. At Hartwick Seminary, of 12 candidates for the ministry, one-half are supposed to be self-supporting and one-half beneficiaries. [Estimated.] Of 52 theological students in the Philadelphia Seminary, 32 are self-supported, and 20 are sustained by different synods. Of 43 candidates in Muhlenberg College, 23 are supported by themselves, and about 20 by the synods. In Thiel College, out of 35 candidates for the ministry, 23 are self-supporting, and 12 beneficiaries. In Augustana Seminary, at Rock Island, there are 36 theological students, and in the college about 50 candidates, all of whom are supported by the churches, but pay their own tuition. Of 10 theological students in the Seminary at Salem, Va., but 2 are self-supported and 8 are beneficiaries. Of 13 candidates for the

ministry in Roanoke College, 4 are self-supported, and 9 receive
aid from the Church and the college. In Newberry College, S.
C., there are 8 candidates, 5 of whom are self-supported, and 3
are beneficiaries. Of 59 theological students in the Mendota
Seminary, and 17 candidates for the ministry in the Gymnasium
of the German Synod of Iowa, hardly any are supported by
their parents, and nearly all are sustained by the churches. Of
39 students in the Seminary at Columbus, O., 13 are self-supported, and 26 are beneficiaries, and of 45 candidates for the
ministry in Capital University, 17 are self-supported, and 31 are
assisted by the Synod of Ohio. Of 105 theological students in
the Concordia Seminary, at St. Louis, about two-thirds, or 70,
are self-supported, and one-third, or 35, assisted by the churches,
and of 184 theological students in the Pro-Seminary at Springfield, Ill., about two-thirds or 192 support themselves, and one-
third or 97 are supported by the churches, and of 200 candidates for the ministry in the Gymnasium at Fort Wayne, and
114 in the Pro-Gymnasia about one-half, or 157 are self-supported, and the other half, or 157, are supported by congregations, and the general beneficiary fund. Total, 349 who educate
themselves, and 254 who are educated by the Missouri Synod.

The following summary exhibits the proportion of the theological students in the seminaries, and the candidates for the
ministry in the colleges who are supported by their parents and
those who are sustained by the Church in the several ecclesiastical bodies mentioned above. In the institutions of the General Synod (North) of 173, 87 are self-supporting, and 86 are beneficiaries. In those of the General Council—not including the
Swedish Augustana Synod—of 120 students, 78 are self-supporting, and 52 are beneficiaries. In the Swedish Augustana
Synod there are 85 theological students and candidates all of
whom are supported by the churches—their tuition excepted.
In those of the General Synod (South) of 31 candidates for the
ministry, 11 are self-supported and 20 are beneficiaries. In those
of the Joint Synod of Ohio, there are 87 candidates of whom 30
are self-supported and 57 beneficiaries. In those of the German
Synod of Iowa there are 76 candidates, nearly all of whom are
supported by the churches. And of 603 candidates for the

ministry in the institutions of the Missouri Synod 349 support themselves and 254 are sustained by congregations and the general beneficiary treasury.

Revivals of religion have marked the development of the Church in America. They consist of the simultaneous conversion of many persons, under the appropriate use of the appointed means of grace. And although unscriptural methods have been resorted to in promoting them, and spurious religious excitements have abounded, genuine revivals constitute the promised seasons of refreshing from the presence of the Lord, and their fruits, tried by the tests of Scripture, will compare favorably with those gathered through the regular preaching of the word and the instructions of the youth in the catechetical class. The bearing of revivals of religion cannot therefore be overlooked in the discussion of our subject.

In revivals many persons are converted in a comparatively short period of time, a due proportion of whom are young men. The first impulses of the new born soul are characterized by benevolence, prompting to usefulness. The claims of the ministry are frequently presented, at such times, in various forms by ministers and others, and the question of highest usefulness decided by many in its favor.

This is especially the case in college revivals, where the subjects are all young men, most of whom have not yet determined, in the light of conscience and the word of God, what their life-work shall be. It was our privilege to preach series of discourses, five times to the students of Pennsylvania, three times to those of Wittenberg, and once to those of Roanoke College, in which about three hundred young men turned unto the Lord, more than one hundred of whom devoted themselves to the ministry, and the majority of them are still alive and doing good service in the cause of Christ. The examples cited by Prof. Tyler in his Prize Essay on Prayer for Colleges, prove beyond all cavil the importance and value of college revivals, in replenishing the ranks of the ministry.

Ministers, as spiritual fathers and the religious teachers of the people, render them the most useful and valuable service, and deserve at their hands the highest consideration. Accordingly the Scriptures enjoin upon all the members of the Church to esteem their pastors very highly, to receive "with meekness the ingrafted word," to submit to their rule in the Lord, to coöperate with them in every good word and work, and to pray for, and to render them a just and adequate support. And while the performance of each of these duties will add something to the comfort and usefulness of a pastor, the combined result of obeying them all will be to invest the ministerial office with its legitimate functions, rights and emoluments, and exhibit it in its true and scriptural light. Just in proportion as this is done, will the office of the ministry appear desirable and attractive to young men, and just in proportion as the ministry is regarded with disrespect, its counsels unheeded, its authority despised, and its support stinted, will the office appear repulsive and young men be deterred from entering it. When such unjustifiable burdens are added to the ordinary privations and trials of the ministry, it is not to be wondered at that the office must go begging, and that the great majority of thoughtful young men can without compunction of conscience disregard the command of Christ: "Son, go work to day in my vineyard." And as the prosperity of the Church depends upon the number and character of her ministers, their proper treatment or their cruel neglect become important factors in determining the measure of the supply and the extent of the deficiency in the ranks of the ministry. And a proper regard for or disregard of the ministers affects God himself, who, while he promises to call an adequate number of laborers into the harvest, on condition, involving the proper treatment of his servants, he on the other hand threatens to remove the candlesticks from the churches that refuse to hear, honor and maintain his messengers, as the lights of the world.

The bearing of the inadequacy of ministerial support, upon the supply of the ministry, is so direct and telling, that we cannot forbear calling attention to it. God made ample provision for the maintainance of the priests and the levites, and Christ declared that the laborer was worthy of his hire, and that those who preach the Gospel should live from the Gospel. And yet, so little are the principle and command of Christ heeded by the

churches, that the great majority of ministers obtain an inadequate support, and but few receive such salaries as to be able to
provide for themselves and families during their active service,
as well as when disabled by sickness and the infirmities of age.
And the effect of this injustice, and consequent want and suffer-
ing, upon parents and their gifted sons is such, that fathers are
tempted to dissuade their sons from choosing, and the sons from
considering the claims of the ministry.

The following extract from the letter of Dr. John Hall, called
out by the threatened famine of the ministry in the Presbyterian Church, is strikingly in point here :

"We are a people growing in wealth more rapidly than any
other. We have our largest church served by a ministry with
an average income of about $500 a year. We have thrown
away the principle and the burdens of an "establishment," and
we have a clergy in whose straits and privations the writer of
touching columns finds the readiest material for rousing cheap
sympathy.

"We in the religious world are lamenting—I had almost said
whining—over a deficient supply of candidates for the ministry,
and we are making things artificially and unhealthily easy for
such as come; and side by side with our joy over ten millions
of communicants is the pitiful tale of domestic distress and
pinching poverty in the homes of those who minister to these
millions.

We invite the sons of such men as can educate their boys at
their own cost, as physicians, lawyers, artists, engineers, sometimes sending them to Europe for greater advantages—we invite them to the ministry, practically telling them in our literature and our life that we shall reckon closely the minimum on
which they can live, and "retire" them without pension when
they have passed their prime. And we wonder that they do
not come to our seminaries. We may tell them, indeed, that
the disciple has to take up his cross; but the average American
youth has sense enough to know that ministers are not specially
singled out for the cross; that it is for all; and that it is possible to serve God faithfully without being in the ministry. And

so they stay away, and we have to adopt exceptional methods
to draw good and educated men into this profession."

Of the same tenor are the following remarks made by Dr.
Thomas Guthrie :

"The calamity which I stand in dread of, and which is next to
the withdrawal of the divine blessing, the greatest a church can
suffer, is that the rising talent, genius, and energy of our country may leave the ministry of the Gospel for other professions.
'A scandalous maintenance,' Matthew Henry says, 'makes a
scandalous ministry.' And I will give you another equally
true. 'The poverty of the parsonage will develop itself in the
poverty of the pulpit.' I have no doubt about it. Genteel
poverty, to which some ministers are doomed, is one of the
great evils under the sun. To place a man in circumstances
where he is expected to be generous and hospitable, to open
his hand as wide as his heart to the poor, to give his family
good education, to bring them up in what is called genteel life,
and to deny him the means of doing so is enough, but for the
hope of heaven, to embitter existence.

"In the dread of debt, in many daily mortifications, in harrass-
ing fears what will become of his wife and children when his
head lies in the grave, a man of cultivated mind and delicate
sensibilities has trials to bear more painful than the privations of
the poor. It is a bitter cup, and my heart bleeds for brethren
who have never told their sorrows, concealing under their cloak
the fox that gnaws at their vitals."

In natural husbandry, the forces of nature must be brought
into contact with the germ or life force in order to secure ger-
mination, growth and fructification. And analogy requires the
same procedure in spiritual husbandry. In order that the
Spirit may call a soul into the kingdom of God, through a supernatural begetment and spiritual birth, it becomes indispensable that the truth, as the incorruptible seed of regeneration be
brought, by the Church, in contact with the mind, heart, conscience and will in the formation of a new creature in Christ
Jesus. For the Church to expect such results, by the direct
inward illumination of the Spirit, without the written word, as
the enthusiasts maintain, would prove a delusion and a snare

and fill her folds with hypocrites and fanatics. Notwithstanding the number and character of the passages, pertaining to the call, qualifications and work of the ministry, contained in the Scriptures, their adaptation so to impress the faculties of the soul as to develop the conviction of a call to the ministry, and the corresponding practice of Christ and the apostles in calling out those who bore the marks of a call, and setting them to work in the kingdom of God, the Church in this country, under the influence of the prevalent theory, has settled down into a state of indifference in regard to the call to and supply of the ministry. Scarcely any interest is taken in the subject, and little or no sense of obligation is felt by any one, to make an intelligent effort to impart information and to endeavor to convince any talented and pious young man of his call to the ministry.

All the agencies of the Church, which ought to be brought into requisition in bringing the truths concerning the call to the ministry, its qualifications and work, in contact with the minds and hearts of young men, are derelict in duty and greatly at fault. In most households God is not recognized at the family altar, and the claims of the ministry are shut out from the consideration of the baptized sons of the Church. In the congregation the prayer : "Lord send forth laborers into thy harvest," is seldom if ever heard in a prayer meeting or in the pulpit; no elder, deacon or member thinks that he has anything to do with looking out for the marks of a call to the ministry in young men, and very few of the largest and wealthiest congregations contribute enough money to sustain regularly even *one* candidate for the ministry. The Sunday-school teacher becomes the substitute of the parents in imparting religious instruction, and the Common School and the State University take the place of the parochial school and the Christian College, in the education of the sons of many church members, and from neither do they ever hear a word about the office of the ministry, and their obligations in regard to it. In the pulpit, discourses on the call to the ministry are seldom, and in many never heard, and all references to it are so tinctured with mystical representations about the call of the Spirit, that no Scriptural impression is made thereby, either on parents, young men, church officers or members.   And the church paper, however highly it might be freighted with instruction on the call to and work of the ministry is voluntarily shut out of tens of thousands of the homes of professed church members, and whose sons never receive a ray of light on this great subject. And while the foregoing presents a glance at the negative side of the subject, its positive side must not be·overlooked. Beneficiary Education, by perversion from its true design, becomes the means of drawing an undue proportion of the sons of poor families into the ministry, and the occasion to the rich to withhold an undue proportion of their sons from the ministry, so that not one of our wealthy and cultured families in a hundred, yea, scarce one in a thousand, has a representative in the ministry of the Church.   So great has the dread of spurious revivals, with their unscriptural methods become, that no prayers are offered and intelligent efforts made to promote genuine ones, and thus these prolific sources of ministerial supply have been cut off. And so inconsiderate and unkind has the treatment of the ministry been on the part of many congregations, so inadequate the salaries paid them, and so onerous the trials and sorrows to which they and their families have been subjected, that the ministerial office, high and noble as it is, has been divested of its true attractions, and is shunned rather than chosen by many gifted and thoughtful young men.   In a word, under the demoralizing influence of the prevalent theory, the ministry receives little consideration anywhere, and is ruled out almost everywhere.   The relative merits of the prevalent and true theories of a call to the ministry are not thoroughly discussed in our theological seminaries, and our ministers are sent out, either with no definite views on the subject, or with mystical and un-Lutheran proclivities.   The professors in our colleges and the teachers in our classical preparatory schools, who possess the best opportunities for discovering such gifts of mind, heart and speech, as give promise of adaptation for, and indicate a call to the ministry, do not avail themselves of them, and students, after years of daily intercourse, pass from under their care, without having been spoken to on the subject of the ministry, or its claims as a profession for life urged upon them. And education committees have given so much weight to the account given them by applicants for aid, of the time, place, circumstances and manner in which the Holy Spirit called them to the ministry, that they accept them without demanding such other corroborative evidences as the Spirit requires those to furnish, whom he has called, according to his own testimony given in the Scriptures. And so much veneration have they for this mystic call of the Spirit, and so much do they stand in dread of keeping one of God's elect out of the ministry, that they continue applicants on the funds from year to year, whose deficiencies of talents, grace and gifts of speech, have become notorious among their class-mates and fellow-students, if not to their teachers in the college and their professors in the seminary. Furthermore, the prevalent theory has paralyzed all the springs of intelligent effort in calling out the elect sons of God into the ministry of the Church, while she has folded her hands, and watched with complacent inactivity for a larger increase in the number of ministers, through the mystic call of the Holy Spirit. The question concerning the call and supply of the ministry has been taken out of the department of the origination and use of adapted means for the attainment of spiritual and ecclesiastical ends, and removed to the sphere of inspiration and of mysticism, in which enthusiasts are engaged in endeavoring to discover by dreamy introspection, the inner call to the ministry. It ought not, therefore, to awaken surprise, that so few of the pious and gifted young men of the Church have entered the ministry, but rather excite wonder that so many have devoted themselves to it; that so large a proportion of them have by their ability, fidelity and success, given full proof of their ministry, and received the divine seal of the legitimacy of their call and investiture of the sacred office.

APPEAL TO THE ELECT YOUNG MEN OF THE CHURCH.

Redemption presents the greatest of all subjects, the Bible is the most wonderful revelation, and the ministry the first of all professions. Its great theme is "Christ and him crucified." Its special work the moral recovery of man. Its ultimate end the

salvation of a lost world. Its Exemplar was Jesus Christ. It
has been graced by prophets and apostles. To its service illus-
trious men "of whom the world was not worthy," have devoted
their lives. In its prosecution martyrs have died. And among
its supernatural associates, angelic messengers as ministering
spirits, sent forth to minister to the heirs of salvation, are found.

The Church is "the pillar and ground of the truth," the bearer
of the redemption powers, designed to recover to holiness and
happiness a ruined world. The Lutheran Church constitutes
the most numerous Protestant branch. Her origin marks the
greatest era of modern history, and her ecclesiastical achievements stamp her with renown. Reorganized after the model of
the apostolic and primitive Church, her distinguishing characteristics doctrinal, liturgical, governmental and ceremonial, place
her mid-way between ecclesiastical extremes, and, in their com-
bination and consistent development, constitutes her a great and
glorious Church. And the service to which she calls her sons
is, therefore, at once, the most interesting, useful, happifying
and ennobling, and the field of labor to which she invites them
in America, is wider in extent, richer in material, and more
promising in results, than that opened to the sons of any other
denomination in this land. God by creation has conferred upon
hundreds and thousands of the young men in the Lutheran
Church, the natural talents, by Redemption, the spiritual graces,
and by Providence, furnished the means and opportunity to prepare themselves for the work of the ministry. The considerations presented to them in this article, prove that the question
of vocation must be determined by highest usefulness, and as
the ministry stands unrivaled in this respect, those endowed
with the necessary qualifications, bear the marks of the call to
the ministry, and are morally bound to devote themselves to it.
Upon the conscience of all such, we lay, with mountain weight,
the call of the Lord of Glory to enter the great harvest, and assist in gathering it into the garner of heaven.

Let them not magnify its labors and trials, nor overestimate
its difficulties, but let them study its claims, until, with Paul,
they are constrained to cry out, "Necessity is laid upon me, yea,
woe is me if I preach not the Gospel." Let them not consult

with flesh and blood, but respond to the Master's call, prepare thoroughly for his work, prosecute it with fidelity and perseverance, bear hardness as good soldiers of the cross, and they will enjoy the approbation of conscience, the esteem of men, and the favor of God. And, finally, after a triumphant death, they will be recognized and greeted, at the general resurrection, as the deliverers of those whom they were instrumental in bringing to the knowledge of the truth ; and in presenting them as the trophies of their ministerial labors, each one may exultingly exclaim: "Here, Lord, am I, and children that thou hast given me," to which he will respond: "Well done, good and faithful servant; thou hast been faithful over a few things, I will make thee ruler over many things, enter thou into the joy of thy Lord." "They that be wise, shall shine as the brightness of the firmament; and they that turn many to righteousness as the stars for ever and ever."

ERRATA.

Page 10 line 5, for "*prevailing*" read "*preaching.*"
Page 24 line 5, for "*teaching*" read "*preaching.*"
Page 24 line 13, for "*that in the word*" read "*the preaching of the word.*"
Page 65 line 2, for "*culcable*" read "*culpable.*"